Shattered

Shattered

J. M. White

COSMIC
EGG
BOOKS

Winchester, UK
Washington, USA

JOHN HUNT PUBLISHING

First published by Cosmic Egg Books, 2019
Cosmic Egg Books is an imprint of John Hunt Publishing Ltd., 3 East St., Alresford,
Hampshire SO24 9EE, UK
office@jhpbooks.com
www.johnhuntpublishing.com

For distributor details and how to order please visit the 'Ordering' section on our website.

Text copyright: J. M. White 2018

ISBN: 978 1 78904 058 6
978 1 78904 059 3 (ebook)
Library of Congress Control Number: 2018934824

A CIP catalogue record for this book is available from the British Library.

Design: Stuart Davies

UK: Printed and bound by CPI Group (UK) Ltd, Croydon, CR0 4YY
US: Printed and bound by Thomson-Shore, 7300 West Joy Road, Dexter, MI 48130

We operate a distinctive and ethical publishing philosophy in
all areas of our business, from our global network of authors to
production and worldwide distribution.

For my brother, Dan.

Chapter 1

Dayna had driven about forty minutes south of Boston at a steady eighty miles per hour before deciding enough was enough and taking the next exit. She decided to check into the first motel she came to, The Green Garden Motel.

It didn't matter where she stayed; rage controlled her now. She never thought her husband capable of an affair. Sure, other people's husbands, but not Richard. His face flashed before her: his wrinkled brow, his smirk of pleasure as he thrust into that other woman in *their* bed, the bed they had shared for twenty-six years.

But his moaning had been the worst part. A gross, guttural sound Dayna had never heard him utter when making love to her. Her fingers tightened on the steering wheel before throwing the car in park and making her way towards the motel office.

Her knuckles were still white from gripping the steering wheel on the drive. They gleamed as she took the flimsy, plastic key card from the greasy man behind the counter. He wore a nametag that read: MICK and underneath that: HAPPY TO HELP. She guessed the latter was a lie.

Dayna found her room with little effort. Room 42, first floor. It was horrid. A dingy, flowered bedspread clashed with the plaid curtains. It reeked of cigarettes despite the NO SMOKING sign. The pine green carpet looked recently vacuumed, but probably hadn't seen a replacement in twenty years, maybe more. With no bags to unload, she walked to what she presumed to be the mini bar. The small fridge smelled faintly of bleach, but it had what she wanted. Vodka. She downed two nips.

Sitting on the bed, she began to cry. She felt pathetic. On the drive, she had reached one conclusion and right now, she was damn sure of it. There are only two types of middle-aged women in this world. According to Hollywood, there are the ones who

1

are still thought of as attractive. The ones who have spectacular sex and extramarital affairs because they have an abundance of men to choose from. The ones who are pushed against walls and fucked at impossible angles.

Then, there are the forgotten ones. Like her. They get up every morning and study the progression of age in the mirror, utilizing expensive anti-aging lotions, potions, and pills, trying to prevent the inevitable. They're the ones who lack any sexual presence, living as motherly figures, while the men their age lust after twenty-year-olds with tight, perky butts.

The memory surfaced again: her husband at the foot of the bed. The tail of his shirt flapping over his bare ass, his slacks around his ankles and a bright turquoise thong resting by his shoe. A topless woman hinged across the bed in front of him, her black pencil skirt bunched up around her lower back. The girl's long, blond hair cascading past her ears, brushing the bedspread. Dayna had stared at her breasts as they swung in time to Richard's thrusts. As she remembered, the woman—girl—couldn't have been older than twenty-five.

Dayna shivered, and any trace of sadness dissipated into a violent rage. Losing all composure, she grabbed a third nip from the mini bar, drained it and whipped it at the wall. She ripped the pillows from the bed and threw them around the room. A hanging picture clattered to the floor. Tears streamed down her face as she screamed and pounded on the bed. Unsatisfied, she slammed her right fist into the wall as hard as she could. After her third punch, she stopped, catching a glimpse of herself in the large mirror hung above the dresser.

She walked forward, mesmerized by her reflection. She barely recognized the wild woman who stared back. Her pulse pounded in her ears as warm blood dripped from her knuckles. Her cheeks were wet with tears, eyes blackened from mascara, hair disheveled. She hated herself, but she hated Richard even more. A feeling of utter desperation flowed through her as if carried by her veins, a feeling so strong, it overpowered her.

A flicker of movement caught her attention. It was a momentary lapse of light, as if someone had crossed behind her. She whirled around, half expecting to see greasy Mick from the front desk grinning at her.

Nothing. The room was empty.

Now, she no longer felt like a ruined middle-aged woman, but a scared little girl.

Stress. It was clearly stress. Stress can do strange things to a person; she'd heard the stories. She just needed to calm down, maybe splash some cool water on her forehead.

In the bathroom, the soft buzzing of the cheap fluorescent lights calmed her in a way she couldn't explain. Taking a deep breath, she leaned over the sink and splashed cold water onto her face.

Richard surfaced once more, with eyes wide and mouth agape. He had spotted her watching them from across the bedroom. He'd shoved the girl away from him and she shrieked. He'd whirled around, making a pathetic attempt to shield his genitals from Dayna's sight, then grabbed for his pants. Fumbling to latch his belt, he stepped towards her. "It's not what you think," he had said. Or at least that's what Dayna thought he had said. It had been difficult to hear over the drumming of her heart.

She splashed her face with more water and reached up blindly, feeling for a towel, and brought it to her face before straightening. The cheap fabric was scratchy against her skin. As she removed the towel and gazed into the mirror, her eyes widened in surprise, then fear. A black figure peered back at her. It appeared womanly but lacked any real detail. Its presence, however, was dark, utterly negative.

Dayna spun around. Nothing! Her hand dropped and jittered by her side. Hoping her eyes were playing tricks on her, Dayna turned back to the mirror. The figure had returned. It was now directly behind her, close enough to reach out and grab her. It wore a hooded cloak that cast a shadow over most of its face, distorting any features. Only its eyes were exposed, eyes unlike any she'd seen before. The whites were a stormy grey and the pupils black as coal. God only knew what kind of creature lurked underneath the rest of that hood.

The figure lunged forward within the glass and let out a raspy scream. Dayna jumped back terrified, falling into the tub. Grabbing at the shower curtain, she tore the cheap plastic liner from the rings and regained her footing. She charged out of the bathroom, running for the front door where her trembling hands fought with the unfamiliar locks.

She managed to break free into the parking lot and lock herself inside her car. Panting, she began to cry. What the hell had she seen? She jammed her key into the ignition and tore out of the gravel parking lot.

Chapter 2

Dayna eyed the speedometer, wrestling with the desire to max the Chevy out at 160. There was no reason to run. That thing in the motel was nothing to be concerned with. She was writing it off as stress. Dayna liked a good horror movie now and again, but she didn't believe in ghosts. After all, she'd managed to make it forty-eight years without ever seeing one. Today was no different. That figure wasn't a ghost, it was her mind getting the best of her and she'd be stupid to think otherwise. It didn't stop her hands from shaking though.

She pulled into the driveway and parked behind Richard's white Porsche. *You can do this. You can't run forever,* she reminded herself.

"Dayna?" Richard called to her as soon as she shut the front door.

She slipped off her heels and took a deep breath. In the dining room, she found an anxious Richard pacing, glass of whiskey in hand. The table had been set. A pot roast surrounded by glazed carrots and potatoes sat at his end of the table. Carving fork and knife were at the ready. Candles in the center. A brimming martini glass beside her plate.

It would have been a nice gesture if his pot roast could make up for his infidelity.

He approached her, a desperate half-smile on his face. She folded her arms in front of her chest, as much to conceal her trembling hands as to stand her ground.

"Dayna, honey, we need to talk."

She said nothing.

"What happened earlier was a mistake. I swear it. You shouldn't have had to see that."

She glared at him. For Christ's sake, he wasn't really sorry, just sorry he'd been caught. Did he expect *her* to apologize for ruining his fuck session?

He held out his hands. "You mean everything to me, if I could take it back I would. I guess... I guess I was just lonely."

Lonely? She clenched her jaw. If anyone had the right to be lonely it was her. She was home all day while he worked. Her life revolved around him. Fresh coffee for his mornings. Dinner ready for seven o'clock. Dressed to the nines to accompany him to his silly functions. Sure, she had the luxury of working from home, something some women might envy. But with it came debilitating loneliness. She'd hinted at that before, but he'd always treated her complaint with disinterest.

He stepped toward her. "Please say something, Dayna... anything?"

"Stay away from me, Richard," she said. "What would you like me to say? That I forgive you?" When he began to stutter something useless, she cut him off. "Well, I don't."

"Dayna, please. We have a child together, a life together—"

"And now, all of a sudden, you care about that. The time to care was before you stuck your dick in some twenty-year-old." She raised her voice." I'm not good enough for you, is that it? Too old?"

"No. No. I—"

"How long Richard? Huh? How long has this shit been going on?"

He took a long, slow drink from his glass.

"Answer me," she said.

"Two," he muttered.

"Jesus, speak up!"

"Two years."

She almost staggered, as if hit in the chest by a bowling ball. She looked down, boring her eyes into the carpet.

"Dayna, I'm so sorry—"

"Were there others?" she asked.

"What?"

"Others."

He offered a painful look. "She's not... "He sighed. "One. It happened at a conference. Just once, I swear. Maybe... I don't know, seven years ago. It was so long ago, Dayna. It was a mistake."

Once a cheater, always a cheater echoed through her mind. "I see," she whispered.

"What do you want, Dayna?" He raised his voice. "A divorce?" She held her tongue.

"What do you want me to do?" he yelled.

"I don't want you to do anything. You've done enough already," she said. Grabbing his failed olive branch of a martini from the table, she turned her back on him and headed for the stairs.

She ignored his desperate shouts as he followed her. On the first step, she paused, wanting to toss the glass in his face. But what good would that do? "Stay down here," she said. "I'm done talking."

At the door to her bedroom she hesitated. It was almost incomprehensible: Richard... his slut... in *her* room. She glared at the bed with loathing. "And find somewhere else to sleep," she yelled back to him before slamming the bedroom door.

On her way to the bathroom, she found herself avoiding the spot where they'd been doing it. She stopped and studied the bed once more. The girl's hands had been *right there*. Her fury exploding, she yanked off the sheets, dragged them into the bathroom, and tossed them into the tub. She removed a match from the box beside the candles on the windowsill, lit it, and held it to the corner of the sheets. Sipping her martini, she watched with satisfaction as the flames spread across the fabric. The smoke detector blared, the flames crackled, and a black figure loomed within the mirror behind her.

Chapter 3

It seemed that only a few days later, her life had been changed for good. Mornings that once started with the gym and a green smoothie now started with a cold shower and a Vicodin. It was definitely not a positive change, nothing that would be recommended by doctors, but it did the job.

The distant slam of a door brought Dayna back to the present. She suppressed a twitch, Richard must be leaving for work. Her eyes fluttered open as she became aware of the hot water running down her head and trailing down her back. Reaching for her bottle of potent lavender body wash, she squirted a generous amount into her hands and created a lather. She cupped her hands together, brought them to her nose and took a deep inhalation, hoping the lavender would calm her. She played that game a lot lately, pretending something would relax her, give her some peace of mind. Tea instead of coffee. A glass of warm milk before bed. Yet the only thing that really did the trick was a good glass of wine—or two.

She had been in the shower for about twenty minutes now. She'd stay another five, giving Richard enough time to gather his coffee, granola bar, and keys. She waited for the rumbling sound of the garage door lifting before turning the shower to its coldest setting and relishing the feeling of the icy water on her skin.

She turned off the shower, stepped out and used a towel to pat-dry. Rubbing was a no, no. Rubbing caused wrinkles. Leaving the bathroom, she watched the steam rush to escape into the cooler bedroom air. She snatched her black bathrobe from behind the door and seated herself at her vanity. Something she had found off Craigslist, the vanity was carved from mahogany and painted white with a slight distressed style. It had a beautiful mirror that was now covered by one of her black scarfs in an attempt to create an illusion of safety. The possibility of glimpsing the dark figure in another mirror made her heart flutter. She knew it was silly, but her mind often wandered back to the motel. You would think it would be the least of her problems. Yet, at night, when she lay in total darkness, her eyes tried playing tricks and her mind jumped to terrifying conclusions—keeping the mirror hidden was an easy solution.

Downstairs, Dayna reached for a banana and sat at her laptop. She stared, zombie like, into the blue screen. She was supposed to be answering the office's emails, but the thick smell of coffee and cologne lingering in the air was distracting. It reminded her of Richard.

Life's funny. She never imagined her marriage would be like this, never would have guessed it in a million years. How could she? Richard was so handsome when he was younger. He had the dignified good looks of an older man even then. George Clooney-esq perhaps. At twenty-two, she was so anxious to get married and start a life with the man she loved, she never even bothered to contemplate the possibility of things going bad. How could she have predicted the downward spiral their relationship would take more than two decades later?

She blinked and yanked her wandering mind back to the looming screen. She needed to answer these emails. Richard's psychiatry work was divided, part of the reason he was a workaholic. He worked part-time as a psychiatrist for McClain's Psychiatric Hospital in Belmont. He also had a private practice in Boston where he saw clients on Thursdays and Fridays. His clients in Boston were the type who paid out of pocket to get their antidepressants because their daughter wouldn't do her homework and they couldn't be sure if their dog liked the color pink. Why else wouldn't Fluffy wear the sweater? For the last fifteen years, her unofficial position was to deal with these types of people as sort of a secretary, answering their insurance questions and cramming them into Richard's two available days.

She gnawed at the end of a pen, a gross habit her mother had always discouraged. Screw the email. She wasn't being paid. Her contribution to Richard's business was a luxury he did not currently deserve.

She opened a new tab and brought up the AT&T website. After logging in, she looked for anything labeled "Call Records" or "Call Details". She wanted to see phone calls and text messages from the last billing cycle. Television, maybe *Law and Order*, had taught her that obtaining your own cell phone records is doable for the average person, no FBI agent needed. However, it was far more challenging than she had anticipated to ferret out the cell records of her husband.

Her investigation was interrupted by a knock at the side door. She was startled by the sound and her own jumpiness annoyed her. Who could it really be? After all, there seemed to be an unspoken rule that the side door was reserved for the people you knew and who had been granted special VIP access. It wasn't used by strangers or murderers; they hardly ever knocked.

She peered through the blinds in the side door's small window. It was Max, her son, twenty-seven come August. She'd miscarried two years after having Max and had always thought of that baby as her son too, but she supposed birth order titles were reserved for the living. She opened the door.

"Hi, honey," she said, giving him a hug and kiss on the cheek. He reeked of cigarettes and aftershave. The cigarettes disappointed her, but she kept her mouth shut. After all, he hadn't even taken his coat off.

"Hi, Mom."

"How's it going?" She smiled. It'd been almost a month since she'd last seen him.

"Can't complain. You look good," he replied.

The statement made her feel uncomfortable. She ran a nervous hand through her blonde hair. Could he tell something was different? That she was different.

She laughed, hoping to bury her anxiety. "Thanks. You on

your way to the station?" He was dressed in his uniform. Dayna always thought he looked handsome in it. Max had been a Boston police officer for almost five years now and the job suited him.

"Yup, I have a few minutes though."

She smiled, regaining her composure. "Coffee?" She already knew the answer and put on a pot.

"Sure."

"How's Becca?"

He took a seat at the table. "She's great. We're doing really well, Mom."

"Good, good." She crossed her arms waiting for the coffee to brew. There was a momentary silence, one she noticed happened often between grown children and their parents. A brief but awkward moment when they both realize they are just two adults asking about each other's days and families, living separate lives and having a conversation they could have with any stranger.

"How's Dad?" he finally asked.

"He's fine." She turned around, fidgeting with the sugar packets in the ceramic dish by the coffee machine, keeping her hands busy kept them from shaking. "You know... same old."

"I haven't heard from him in a while."

Great, so he was neglectful on all accounts. That's consistency for you. "Yeah, he's been busy. Just—well, real busy." The coffee maker hissed, beginning its slow drip of caffeine. Dayna almost sighed in relief.

"So," she said, turning towards him. "Maybe you would know how to do this. I need to access our cell records. I know there's a way to do it, I just don't know how. Technology deficient, you know?" She nudged her laptop towards him, admitting defeat. "I think the page is already open."

"Yeah, sure. Why do you need that?"

"I just—your father lost one of his client's numbers. He needs it for Monday," she said, hating to lie.

"Yeah, no problem."

For just a second, she thought she saw a look of doubt cross his face, but he grabbed her laptop anyway. After all, what son told his mother no?

By the time she slid his coffee in front of him, cream no sugar, he already had the information up on the screen.

"You just need to click on primary account holder." He turned the screen towards her pointing to the upper right-hand corner. "Select the number you want to access, then account history. Easy as that." She nodded, pretending to care.

"Need anything else?"

"No, I'll take it from here," she said.

Fifteen minutes later, after Max had chugged his coffee and left, Dayna sat back down in front of the laptop. There, displayed in front of her, was a little glimpse into Richard's world. Six months' worth of dates, times, and corresponding numbers were laid out before her. *617-234-5567.*

The number was scattered everywhere, usually called around 6:00 p.m., but sometimes 10:00 or 11:00 pm. He didn't seem to discriminate between days either. He called it on Tuesdays, Thursdays, Fridays, even weekends. Richard never called clients on weekends.

Dayna could feel her heart pumping, fueled by a wicked combination of anger, anxiety, and caffeine. The number hadn't been called in the last week. She wasn't sure what that meant but reached for her phone anyway. She punched the number in, ensuring she copied it correctly. She pressed the green phone button and held it to her ear, a tremor in her hand.

It rang. On the fourth ring a woman answered, "Hello?"

She sounded like she had rushed to answer the phone.

She sounded young.

She sounded pretty.

Dayna hung up.

Chapter 4

Dayna had dinner ready by 7:00 p.m. as she always did. Richard joined her after suggesting that they *try* dinner tonight, giving her a patronizing thumbs-up when she had reluctantly agreed.

Now they were sitting, almost defiantly, across from one another, with the long dining table spanning between them. She had even lit some candles as if ambiance was the answer to their problems.

Dayna amused herself through most of dinner by imagining a normal couple enjoying a meal: the talking, the laughing, asking about each other's days. But here, there was only silence. No talking. No noise, other than the chewing of food and soft clinking of silverware. Richard might have cleared his throat once, breaking the quiet, and she had glanced up eager, hoping he was choking.

A good fifteen minutes passed before Richard stood, muttered a thank you and cleared his plate. She finished the rest of her meal alone.

That night she lay in bed motionless, her hands folded over her chest like a corpse. She tossed and turned for over an hour. At one point, she heard Richard's heavy footsteps pass by the bedroom door as he made his way down the hall.

She glanced at the clock—twelve minutes since the last time check—and resumed staring at the ceiling. Nights were always the hardest. She couldn't avoid replaying the disaster with Richard over and over, like a horrible late-night infomercial selling something she didn't need. It always started the same, with Richard thrusting into that girl as her long, golden hair brushed the duvet on the bed that Dayna was currently trying to sleep in. And it always ended in the motel where she had seen those ghostly eyes peering back at her from the mirror.

At some point Dayna had managed to fall asleep and for the first time she did not awake hours before dawn. Turning on to her side, she reached for the orange pill bottle on her nightstand. She popped two of the Vicodin Richard had been prescribed last year, after a minor ankle surgery, before jumping in the shower.

After her shower, Dayna made her way outside to retrieve the newspaper. The cherry trees had already bloomed. Wind had knocked the blossoms to the ground creating a pale pink carpet under her feet. It made her feel like Glenda the Good Witch as she walked down the driveway.

It was sixty-eight degrees, beautiful for April. As a native of Massachusetts, she had long ago decided April was the most unpredictable month, March a close second. Some days were sunny and seventy, other days the ground was frozen and covered in a thick blanket of snow.

She retrieved the paper from the driveway. The protective plastic warm in her hand. Dayna looked up and down the street. The neighborhood was disgustingly quiet, always was. Newton was one of those suburbs where everyone's grass was manicured to perfection. Each lawn marked by a little, yellow square stating CAUTION: HARMFUL PESTICIDES IN USE, below it a slash drawn through thick, black letters spelling 'children' and 'pets'. She often wondered what the point was. Why have such beautiful grass if you were forbidden to go on it in fear of developing some strange cancer? Yet, her lawn sported the same ominous yellow square.

Although only a stone's throw away from downtown Boston, Newton lacked the energy and sounds of the city. Like much of Massachusetts it was old, but charming. Their house and much of the neighborhood was built in 1919, million-dollar homes of old stone, brick and stucco, with modernized insides and all the latest amenities.

The grass got greener and the houses bigger when you entered the town. There was no litter or dog shit left to smolder in the sun. It was an area known for doctors, lawyers, and the affluent. A place where children could play outside, not that they ever did. Instead, children here were carted from one after-school activity to the next. Mandarin to piano, piano to soccer, soccer to tutoring. Little robots kept busy, always pushed to be better. She felt sorry for them.

A flash of brown appeared in her right periphery. A young girl was on the opposite sidewalk, walking towards her with some sort of red cord trailing behind. She was moving like a zombie, her stride slow and crocked, almost like she'd indulged in one too many.

The girl wandered closer. It was Abigail Bailey, or Abby as she preferred. The Bailey family lived five houses down from Dayna, a happily married couple with three kids. She and Richard received their Christmas card each year, which allowed them to watch the Bailey children they'd known since infancy grow up in front of their eyes. Dayna did a quick calculation: Abby would probably be almost thirteen now. But the girl across from her was not the bubbly girl Dayna remembered. Abby's head was down, her small arms crossed around her stomach.

"Abby?" Dayna called. The girl halted, looked toward her, then bent over, hands on knees. Dayna recognized the posture instantly: the girl was about to lose her lunch.

"Abby," she called again, darting across the street towards the girl, her motherly instincts kicking into high gear. Dayna crouched beside her. "Are you all right?"

Abby tilted her face towards Dayna's. Her eyes were wet with tears. "Charlie," she said, her voice breaking. "I need help. He's too heavy. I can't carry him."

Dayna took Abby by the shoulders and gently urged her to stand up straight. A red smear dirtied the front of the girl's light blue shirt. Dayna's heart quickened, but she managed to keep her voice level. "Abby, who is Charlie?"

Abby continued to sob. Instead of answering, she offered

Dayna the red cord she was holding. It was a dog's leash.

A yellow labrador puppy had made his big appearance on the Bailey's Christmas card four months ago. The dopey innocence in the dog's eyes had made Dayna's heart melt and crave a dog of her own. Now, her heart flip-flopped. "Charlie's your dog, isn't he?" she said. "Abby, what's wrong? What happened to Charlie?"

"He got off his leash. I didn't... I didn't mean... and the car, it kept driving. They didn't even stop." Abby's voice quivered. She broke into tears, looking up at Dayna with guilt heavy in her eyes.

"It's not your fault, honey. It's not your fault." Dayna responded in a quiet voice, her hand rubbing Abby's back. Charlie was most likely dead and Abby had witnessed the whole, terrible incident. "Come on, let's get you inside."

Abby shook her head. "No, I can't go back without my dog. I can't... "She stepped away from Dayna. "He's too heavy. I dragged him to the side, but I couldn't—"

"It's okay. I'll get him," Dayna said. "Don't worry. But first we need to get you home." She wrapped an arm around Abby's waist and held her close as they made their way back towards the Bailey's house. Abby shuddered every so often and Dayna put her mouth to the top of her head and whispered, "It's okay," until she calmed down.

At the Bailey's front door, Dayna rang the bell, supporting the weight of a child who would never be the same. Most likely, this day would haunt Abby for the rest of her life.

Pam Bailey opened the door. Taking one look at the two of them, she crouched and held Abby by the shoulders. "Abby, what happened? What happened, darling?" Her eyes found Dayna's when Abby didn't respond.

"Charlie."

"Ran away?"

Dayne shook her head. "I'm sorry."

Pam's face fell. "No," she said. "Where? How—"

"Traffic accident. A car, Abby said. I'll go back and get him."

Pam gathered Abby in her arms. Mother and daughter were both weeping. Dayna stood, watching silently. After a moment, she cleared her throat. "Sorry, but... Abby, where?"

Abby lifted her head from her mother's chest and pointed down the street towards the main road.

"Which way, honey?" Dayna asked. "Toward the park?"

Abby nodded.

"I'll be back soon," Dayna whispered.

Later that afternoon, her sad task completed, Dayna stood at the kitchen counter holding a mug of coffee, looking out the window at the back garden. The crocuses had bloomed last week and the green stems of the daffodils would sport flowers in a few days.

Her cell phone buzzed on the counter. She glanced down at the screen. Richard. Shit.

Aside from last night's dinner, they'd barely spoken since the incident. Still cohabitating, their relationship now consisted of awkward hellos and how-are-yous. Sticky notes instead of direct communication, like two new roommates on opposite shifts. Civil with one another, but the niceties ended there.

Somehow, the incident with Charlie, so unfortunate, so final, made Dayna question her resolve. The display of love and comfort between Pam and Abby caused her to think of her own marriage. She'd loved Richard once, hadn't she? And he her, she was sure of it. Perhaps, she should give him the second chance he had groveled for. Besides, she didn't want a divorce, not really. As Richard had said, "they had a life together." A divorce would be too messy, too disappointing, and they'd been married for too long, so what was the point in being angry. She listened to the voicemail.

Hi, it's me. I don't know if you remember, I know it's last minute but we have that thing at Greg and Monica's tonight. I know it's not the best time, but they're expecting us. Some of my colleagues will be there... I don't know, I think it's at eight. Just think about it, okay? I'll see you later.

His voice came out in a nervous plea, his breathing fast. The result was not like the cool and collected message he had probably intended to convey.

She'd completely forgotten about Greg and Monica. They were throwing some unnecessarily extravagant party. Richard had known Greg for over twenty years. They'd met as undergrads and eventually entered the psychiatry doctoral program together at Boston University. As long as Dayna had known Richard, Greg had been there too. An all-American, always the life of the party, kind of guy. He met Monica sometime in their thirties and from that moment forward they'd become their "couple" friends. Monica was nice enough if you liked a money flaunter. Dayna, personally, did not.

She stared into her half-empty mug. The coffee wasn't hitting the spot. It was just after two. Richard wouldn't be home until after six, and the party started another two hours after that, plenty of time. She opened the fridge, shoving aside a carton of orange juice revealed a bottle of white wine. She poured herself a sizable glass before getting to work on the green bean casserole she wanted to make for the Bailey's. Maybe, if she had enough time, she'd even make some of her famous brownies for Abby. She took a sip of wine and stood a moment longer while looking out at the garden.

Chapter 5

By 7:45 Dayna had nearly polished off the bottle of wine, having her last glass with dinner after dropping off the casserole and brownies at the Bailey's house. The day had been a tough one, but the brownies made Abby smile and that was good enough for her.

She still had a decent buzz as she climbed into Richard's shiny, white Porsche. The party was only fifteen minutes away, but she was glad Richard had decided to take the wheel, not that he'd let her drive the Porsche anyway.

She turned and placed her chin in her hand, resting her elbow on the window's edge and stared through the glass like a bored child on a lengthy road trip. Her mind hazy from intoxication, she could still taste the wine's leftover sweetness on her tongue – *maybe traces of honey dew? Papaya?*

She flinched when Richard placed his hand on her thigh. The skin above her knee was exposed and she had the urge to pull her dress down. For the occasion, she'd chosen a sleek, navy blue dress that fell to her knees. It had a slight V-neck that showed off her cleavage, which she still considered to be one of her better assets.

"It will be fun," Richard assured her, his voice shockingly loud as it cut through the silence. "Maybe even good for us." Now, he only sounded like he was trying to convince himself.

"Yeah," she replied. The mere presence of his hand was making her uncomfortable, but she didn't move it. This was the first step to starting over. After witnessing the love between Pam and Abby, she was determined to make things right. Today, she was a new Dayna, a new wife. She could play it like AA, taking it in small steps and awarding herself a chip for each moment of success. Allowing Richard to keep his hand on her thigh was 'step one' towards a new beginning.

They arrived to find the driveway full and a line of expensive cars parked along the street's edge. Leave it to Monica to invite everybody in town while pissing off her neighbors.

Richard parked the car and dashed around to open her door, likely hoping to score some points. Smiling, he took her hand and lifted her up and out of the car, as if she might break into a thousand pieces if he moved too fast. She muttered a thank you, fighting the urge to roll her eyes. Perhaps that counted as 'step two'?

She walked with him to the door, arm in arm, as good married couples do. Her buzz, unfortunately, had mostly worn off due to the uncomfortable ride. She took a deep breath as they approached the towering mahogany door and let out an audible sigh as Richard rang the doorbell.

Monica swung open the door, as if she'd been perched behind it waiting.

"Dayna! Richard! Thanks for coming. How are you two?" she exclaimed, her voice just a little too high-pitched.

"We're great," Richard replied with an obvious fake enthusiasm.

He leaned in to kiss Monica on the cheek. Looking past them, Dayna saw Greg ambling towards them, shouting, "Richard! Is that you, my man?"

While their husbands were preoccupied with the primitive man-hug, Monica turned to Dayna and held her hands. Dayna peered up at her, always forgetting how tall she was. At six-one it was no surprise Monica had been a model. Not that she'd let you forget it. Most of her conversations somehow turned into past modeling stories, usually beginning with something like, 'Did I ever tell you about my time in Paris?' A glimmer of sadness, oddly beautiful, would appear in her eyes. Such an actress.

"How *are* you, sweetheart?" Monica gushed "It's been *ages*."

It had been, maybe, six months.

Monica had been drinking; Dayna could hear it her voice. She envied her. Especially because Monica was still model-thin, it probably only took two cocktails to get the desired effect. "I'm great, real great," Dayna lied. "How are you?"

The house's décor was modern. A black and white color scheme flowed through each room, punctuated here and there by pops of bright yellow and red. A large, abstract painting of a naked woman spreading her legs was displayed across from the front door. Dayna always pondered what statement Greg and Monica could possibly be trying to make. *Women are beautiful? Peace, love, sex? If you haven't gotten tested, you should?*

The house had five bedrooms and four full baths, much like their own. Despite the size, there were more people than there were seats, huddled in little groups, talking loudly over jazz music. A quick survey of the room proved the people to be much like the house: over the top. The men were in tailored suits and women's dresses had to have cost over six-hundred dollars. The scent of expensive perfumes hung heavy in the air, making her feel sick.

Monica escorted her partway into the room before someone called her name. Monica let out the high-pitch shrill of a high school girl. "Oh my goodness," she squealed. "Dayna, I'll be right back. You know where everything is?" she said before scurrying off.

Dayna shrugged in response to Monica's back. In desperate need of alcohol, she was left to fend for herself. Richard, who had been swept away by Greg, was nowhere to be seen.

The longer she stood still the more she felt a bubble of awkwardness rising around her, surrounding her like a thick, woolen blanket. There was a certain amount of unpleasantness that accompanied parties like these. Richard came from money; she had not. Her father had been a mason, a big, rough man with an aura of whiskey and cigars. A smell, to this day, she found comforting. Her mother, a plump woman with kind eyes, had been a housewife. They were a typical, struggling, blue-collar family.

It wasn't that she couldn't hold her own amongst these people. It was mostly their conversations she dreaded: the dull, uninteresting talk of people who'd never been working-class poor. The women huddled in corners, bragging about their jewelry and marble countertops, while the men talked about sports and the women they wanted to fuck. The few children who got dragged to such parties were ushered away, confined to a bedroom upstairs and forced to be friends, while their parents got plastered and did lines of coke in the bathroom.

Dayna made her way to her favorite part of the house and to what Monica referred to as the parlor. A few summers ago, Monica and Greg had installed an impressive bar and even Dayna had to admit it came out beautifully. A shimmering, white, marble bar top contrasted with dark wood. Hidden within was a large kegerator and full-sized fridge. The bar was always kept fully stocked, one of Monica's better qualities.

As Dayna approached, she wasn't surprised that Monica had hired a bartender for the occasion. She gave her drink order to the under-confident young man behind the bar, who was probably just trying to pay off his mountain of student loans with this part-time gig. She wondered what he had majored in. She wondered how much Monica was paying him and found she felt sorry for the kid. He handed her a chilled glass of white wine with a shy smile.

"Do you take tips?" she asked, handing him a five.

"I'm really not supposed to, I—"

"Well, you do now," she replied, setting the five at the edge of the bar, nudging it towards him.

He scooped it up, squirreling the bill away into his vest pocket and nodded at her.

She smiled.

"Dayna! I thought that was you. You look fabulous!"

She turned from the bar to find Connie McGuire standing behind her. She'd snuck up on her like a wolf hunting deer. Connie was one of Monica's closest friends. If Dayna and Monica went for drinks, Connie always came too. Over time, Dayna had come to like her a lot. The familiar face was a tonic. Sure, Connie was obnoxious but at least she had some personality in comparison to the rest of the crowd.

Connie placed her wine glass on the bar. "Chardonnay," she barked without even looking at the bartender. "Monica said you were coming. I should've known I'd find you at the bar. How are you, darling?"

"I'm good, how —"

"Let me take you to the girls." Connie motioned for Dayna to follow as she snatched her refilled wine glass from the bar without acknowledging the bartender. Acting as if her glass had been magically refilled, she waltzed off, Dayna in tow.

Connie was wearing a bright coral dress. Thin five-inch heels somehow supported her plump figure. Her curled blonde hair was piled into an intricate bun and she was dripping in glittering jewelry: rings, bangles, earrings, and a necklace... the whole shebang. Connie was one of those women who wouldn't be caught looking anything but expensive.

Connie led her toward a group of similar looking woman, Monica at the center. From a distance, their shimmering jewelry made Dayna want to shield her eyes.

"Look who I found," Connie announced, hooking a thumb back over her shoulder.

Monica looked down at the floor, as if she'd forgotten to pick her child up from daycare.

Dayna smiled, greeting each of them. She knew most of them from other parties or outings with Monica. A new face introduced herself as Amy.

Connie took over. "Dayna, Amy's husband is also a psychiatrist. What is his specialty again? Adolescents? Troubled youth?"

As Amy nodded, Connie turned away. Ever the socialite, she'd done her part in the social exchange.

"What a coincidence," Dayna said to Amy, wondering if the woman's husband was also a lousy cheater. Oops! That thought might've knocked her from 'step two' back to 'step one'.

Behind Amy's head hung an oval mirror, providing Dayna with a view of the room. The crowd of people had thinned, most of them migrating towards the bar. Only a few remained, but something wasn't right. Among the men and women huddled behind her was the black shape of the figure. Dayna threw a cautious glance over her shoulder but failed to see the black shape. When she turned her attention back to the mirror, the figure was still there and snapped its head forward.

Dayna's vision tunneled. She stared at it, unable to focus on anything else. The background of jazz music and talking women faded to whispers in comparison to the sound of her own heartbeat. Her wine glass slipped from her hand and shattered. Cool liquid splattered her ankles and up her legs.

"Jesus, Dayna!"

She turned towards the voice. Monica.

"Are you okay, honey? You look pale?"

All the women were staring at her, wearing the same troubled expression. They had each taken a step back to avoid the fallout.

She looked down at her broken glass and the words *party foul* came to her mind for no reason. "I'm sorry. I'm fine, really." Her eyes darted to the now empty mirror, then back to the girls. Connie, who must have noticed, looked briefly over her shoulder, then back at her, raising an eyebrow.

"Too much wine I guess," Dayna said, shrugging as if she'd made a joke.

No one said anything until Connie spoke up. "You're telling me? I'm drunk as a skunk," she boasted. The girls laughed.

"Let me get this," Dayna said, bending down. To do what,

she wasn't sure. Sweep the glass into her bare hands?

"No, sweetie! Don't worry about it," Monica said, taking her by the arm. "The help will take care of it."

Shaking off Monica, Dayna smiled, mentioned the bathroom, and excused herself, only turning back to ask if anyone had seen Richard. They hadn't.

Chapter 6

Dayna searched for Richard with no success. She had to pee, take some deep breaths, and maybe splash some cold water on her face. But most importantly, she wanted to leave. She was already tired of walking and wanted to change out of her wine soaked shoes. She needed her husband. This was good, she actually *needed* Richard, perhaps that bumped her back up the ladder to 'step two', maybe even 'step three'.

Her anxiety heightened as she was greeted by a small line for the bathroom. She let out an audible *are you kidding me* and decided to use one of the upstairs bathrooms instead, wine sloshed in her heels as she climbed the stairs. She felt like she was trespassing, even though she knew Monica wouldn't mind. She couldn't help but think of herself as Belle from *Beauty and the Beast,* entering the castle's forbidden west wing.

By the time she reached the top of the staircase, her nerves had sent her into an awkward jog. She turned the corner, heading down the long hallway to the upstairs bathroom where she came to an abrupt stop.

She'd finally found Richard. He was talking to a young woman in a nice dress, maybe just a little too short for the occasion. For just a moment, it seemed harmless, normal even. The girl started to laugh, batting his chest while twirling a strand of long, blonde hair like a teenager. He laughed in response and wrapped his arms around her waist, his hands too low. Too close to her ass.

It was her! The same long blonde hair falling down her back and off her shoulder; the same breasts that had bounced in sync with Richard's thrusts – probably the same lacey, turquoise thong underneath. Revulsion flooded through her.

A new set of images of her past life with Richard flashed through her head. Smiling up at him on their wedding day. *Flash:* Richard grasping her hand with tears in his eyes as she gave birth to their first son. *Flash:* Them drinking coffee in their pajamas on Christmas morning, watching Max tear open his gifts. *Flash:* Richard holding her as she fell to her knees, gripping her stomach, blood escaping from between her legs, knowing she was miscarrying and losing their second son.

Fleeting last-second images of a marriage milliseconds from death.

Sticky sweat formed on her palms. Tears materialized in her eyes, but she didn't cry. He was such a fucking liar. After promising he would never do it again, here he was, still messing around with this girl right under her nose. Was the temptation of youth really that strong? The joys of reaching 'step three' came crashing down. Richard was back to a big fat zero, a spot he would never be able to slither out of like the snake he was.

"*Leave!*" The voice came from deep inside, a command that cut through her insecurities. She straightened, lifted her chin, and set a new course. She headed down the stairs, pushing past the people in her way, ignoring the group of shiny, shimmering women still huddled where she'd left them.

"Where's the fire?" Connie called.

"Dayna, come back," Monica shouted.

She marched into the street, the sound of her heels harsh against the pavement. Good riddance to them all: fucking Richard, the slut, the worthless friends. She was glad to be free. She slowed to a walk as she passed the Porsche, her initial determination flagging. With no keys and no plan, she called a taxi.

Chapter 7

The Harborside was an upscale bar with an uncreative name in the heart of Boston's seaport district. She had been there once before, about three years ago, with Richard, to celebrate one of his friend's birthdays. Maybe that's why she had blurted out the name when she slid into the taxi, she wasn't sure.

Dayna hesitated at the door. What would people think seeing her enter a bar alone? She couldn't do this, could she? She took a deep breath and entered.

The place had a modern look, was dimly lit and nautically themed. The bar itself was even more appealing, with its shiny granite countertops and backlit high-end liquor. Didn't Grey Goose always look more appetizing when it was illumined?

She was relieved to find an open spot at the bar, where she was greeted by the bartender. He was an older gentleman, closer to her age than the kid back at Monica's that is. He was tall, lean and handsome, although not overly good looking. He placed a cocktail napkin in front of her.

"Whatcha' drinkin'?" he asked in a thick Boston accent.

"How about—just a vanilla martini."

He nodded.

She watched as he crafted her martini in a matter of seconds. Placing the chilled glass in front of her, he made a show of pouring out the alcohol from the shaker into the glass. It always made her uncomfortable when bartenders did that, like they wanted applause or praise. She decided a simple *thank you* would suffice and drank up.

The bartender raised an eyebrow.

She felt the heat of blush. "I was supposed to nurse this, wasn't I?" she said.

He shrugged. "I imagine you needed that."

"As a matter of fact..." She smiled sheepishly. "Any more

where that came from?"

He nodded. No judgment. She liked him.

"I'll take whatever she's having," a voice said to her left.

Dayna looked up, startled. A young man stood beside her, grinning. He was wearing a white button-down shirt and black sport coat. He had dark hair and a little bit of stubble, making him look rugged despite his attire.

"A vanilla martini?" the bartender asked with a hint of skepticism.

"Ah—on second thought, I'll take a whiskey. Straight-up," he said, grimacing. "But, I'm sure she would like another."

"I've already—" she began.

He held up a hand and said to the bartender. "It's on me." He settled onto the stool beside her.

Dayna cleared her throat. Now, how to politely tell him she wanted to be alone? "You don't have to buy me drinks." The statement wasn't exactly polite, but it was direct.

"I don't think I've ever seen you in here before," he said, a slight variation on the traditional opening, ignoring her rejection.

"I know," she said. "First time." She took a sip. The alcohol didn't have quite the hit as the first one.

"I'm here every Wednesday and Friday. Stop by after volunteering at the soup kitchen," he said.

"How kind of you," she said, looking straight ahead at the line of bottles behind the bar.

He chuckled. "It would be if it was true. I just come here after work. A little rest and relaxation to get me through the rest of the week on Wednesdays, and on Fridays, to celebrate getting through the rest of my week. I'm usually with the guys, but you know how it is: no one wants to have a hangover on a workday."

She shrugged. The guy was attempting to be charming. 'A' for effort.

"I doubt you were volunteering at the soup kitchen," he said. "Are you always this well dressed?"

She took a deep breath and let it out. "I just left a party."

He looked at his watch.

She turned to face him. "Skipped out early," she confessed.

"Must have been some shitty party," he said, finishing his drink. "Jimmy!" he called to the bartender. "I'll take another…" He paused, turned, and eyed her almost empty glass. "You know what, we'll both take another!"

"Didn't you hear me?" she asked.

"I know, I know. I don't have to buy you drinks. Too late, though. Done. I'll have to live with my mistake."

She laughed. It had been quite a while since a guy had bought her drinks. It was kind of nice.

"Anyhow," he continued, "we're celebrating."

"Celebrating what?"

"I don't know. New beginnings. New friends. Leaving shitty parties. You pick."

"All right then." She chuckled. "To leaving shitty parties." They clinked glasses and sipped their new drinks.

After finishing her third drink, Dayna was feeling woozy. She swayed in her stool, crossed then re-crossed her legs in an attempt to steady herself. She leaned into the bar and placed her hand under her chin, swiveling her stool towards him. No one wanted to see a forty-eight-year-old woman fall from her bar stool and flail on the sticky wooden floor and she intended to keep it that way.

"I just realized, I don't even know your name," she said, giggling as if she'd made a joke.

"Sam." He smiled and extended his hand. She removed the hand from under her chin and shook his. "Dayna Harris."

"Well it's nice to meet you, Dayna Harris," he replied.

She stared into her empty glass before asking, "So what do you do?" It always came back to small talk it seemed.

"What do I do," he repeated slowly. "Well, I drink," he said, raising his glass in cheers.

She laughed, relieved. Maybe he was starting to feel like her.

"You know that's not what I meant."

"Well, I'm a twenty-six-year-old recent graduate from Suffolk University's master program. I majored in marketing while getting myself in 50,000 plus dollars of debt. Got myself a job at an up and coming marketing agency where I do very little marketing and spend my Friday nights drinking with a lady I don't even know."

She chuckled.

"What about you?"

"What about me?"

"Come on, it's only fair." He signaled to Jimmy for two more drinks

She squeezed her eyes shut for a moment. Jesus Christ, she'd be rolling out of here if she had another. "Well..." she said, focusing on his question. "I live in Newton, right near the Wellesley border."

"Nicer than where I live."

"And where's that?"

"Allston."

"Ah, isn't that where everyone has a nose ring and dirty hair?"

"That's the place all right. Hipster central."

"Hipsters. Right." Embarrassed she didn't know the term, she took a long sip from her new drink, now grateful it had been refilled.

"What do you do for work?" he asked.

"I'm—I don't, ah, not full-time." She grimaced, looking away. That had to sound pathetic. *But what else could she say?* That she answered emails for her prick of a husband that she didn't even speak to as his unofficial, off the books, secretary? Well, she'd certainly given up that job. Retired. She giggled again. If she said *that*, he'd think she was over sixty-five.

"I'm not just some lazy housewife," she said.

"Hey," he said, spreading his hands. "I didn't say—"

"Actually, I work part-time delivering pizzas, have an extensive stamp collection, and own thirty-seven exotic... chihuahuas." Exotic chihuahuas, really? Was that the best she could do?

"Interesting. Now what exactly is an *exotic* chihuahua?"

"Well, they're extremely rare and... very expensive."

"I sense bullshit."

"It's completely true." She laughed, covering her face with her hand.

"Are you married?" he asked, gesturing towards her wedding ring.

The smile fell from her face. "No. Not really."

It felt strange to say it aloud. She shrugged, reaching for her ring as if to hide it, although it was a little too late for that. He nodded a few times and sipped his drink. Her eyes lowered to her glass. She was embarrassed again. Embarrassed by how predictable she was, so depressed by her life and cheating husband that she was drunk at a bar by herself. This boy was not her friend. The word *cliché* echoed in her head.

"Come on," he said, placing his hand on her thigh. "We are celebrating, remember? Nothing's gonna' ruin that."

She smiled. His hand did not make her flinch as Richard's had. Her world did not need to end because Richard, no pun intended, was a dick. Part of her knew this wasn't right, but the other part didn't really care.

"Do you want to get out of here?" she asked, the vodka talking, not her. "I can call us a taxi?"

"My car is parked at the garage down the street."

Chapter 8

Both of them were off their asses drunk, but it didn't stop them from getting into his car. She supposed neither did the risk of getting a DUI or crashing, all those serious consequences seemed impossible while overcome with the euphoria of intoxication.

His car was a shitty, little, green Toyota that reeked of old cigarettes and fast food. Styrofoam coffee cups littered the car's floor amongst other garbage. They crunched under her heels as she lowered herself into the passenger's seat. *Real charming.*

"Sorry about the mess," he said, tossing a few of the Styrofoam cups into the back seat. She could see the embarrassment creep into his eyes.

"It's fine," she replied.

He smiled and began rummaging through a large, black backpack he had taken from the backseat and placed on his lap.

The martinis had left her mind in a vanilla haze, presenting her with only brief moments of clarity, heavy with insecurities. She was too old. This was a bad idea. Her hand hovered over the door handle. She could still leave. And what would her excuse be? That it was past her bedtime and she needed to be getting back to the retirement home? *Get a grip,* Dayna.

Instead, she reached up to pull down the car's visor. Too drunk to care about her current aversion to mirrors.

She gazed into the fingerprint-covered glass. She looked good, but wanted to look better and supposed a little lipstick couldn't hurt.

As she applied a fresh coat of red lipstick, she eyed the lines that covered her neck. There they were, mocking her and laughing as they testified to her true age. She wondered if Sam noticed. She touched the lines, as if rubbing would erase them. For God's sake, she might as well have the number forty-eight tattooed on her forehead.

She caught her breath. In the corner of the mirror she saw it again—the figure. It sat unmoving in the backseat, staring back at her with its dead but knowing eyes.

She shivered as panic took a hold of her. A prickly sensation percolated through her limbs and thin droplets of sweat formed on her palms and forehead. Dayna heard Sam still digging through the backpack's contents, unaware of the danger. She had to take care of this herself. She kept her eye on the figure's reflection while, at the same time, swiveling in her seat prepared to ward off an attack.

One. Two. Three. She whipped around and let out a quiet gasp—the backseat was empty. Vacant of anything besides more trash and clutter. Her eyes scanned every dark corner in the Toyota's interior. She stretched her head over the seat to check the floor. How could that...

"Do you?" Sam asked impatiently.

His voice jolted her back to reality. "What?" Embarrassed, she tried to read his face for any indication that he had seen the dark entity too.

"Do you want to hit this?"

She looked at him puzzled, then at his extended hand. He was offering her a joint. She let her shoulders relax. He hadn't noticed his passenger was a lunatic.

"Why not?" she replied with a faint grin, trying to sound calm and as if partaking in joints with strangers was something she did every day.

She took it from him, her hands still trembling. Holding it as she would a cigarette, she brought it to her lips, working to steady her hands. The joint filled her lungs with a pungent herb-like smoke. The flavor alone made her exhale with a cough. Handing it back to him, she noticed the smudge her red lipstick had left.

The smoke tickled her lungs. She hadn't smoked in more than

a decade. Perhaps the joint would be a pleasant distraction from what she thought she had seen. She raised her eyes and realized the visor was still down with the mirror exposed. She slammed the visor shut and it rattled above her head.

"Jesus, are you all right, Dayna?" Sam asked.

She turned towards him, waving away the swirling smoke that was filling the car.

"I'm fine," she muttered. Sam's eyes were heavy from the pot. Great, the kid was stoned and she was panicked. What a great combination.

"Do you want another hit?" he asked over the soft sound of Led Zeppelin playing on the radio.

Couldn't he see that was the last thing she wanted? Taking what she imagined to be the high road, she replied, "No, I think what I need is another drink."

To her surprise, the alcohol's euphoric effect had faded. Perhaps deathly fear could do that. Her mind had grown clearer and, at the moment, she didn't much like the entire situation. She couldn't let Sam drive. What had she been thinking.

"Ah, I believe I have just the thing," Sam responded. He reached into his backpack of mystery and paraphernalia and pulled out a pint of Jack Daniels like a magician pulling a rabbit from a hat. He took a swig, then leaned over to pass it to her.

"You can't drive like this," she said before taking the bottle.

"I'm fine, really."

She didn't want to be this kid's mother. That was the last thing she wanted, but this was dangerous. She did not want the two of them ending up like Charlie, Abby's poor labrador. Life was short, unpredictable, and she was still the *new* Dayna. "We can take a cab," she suggested.

To her relief, Sam nodded. Now she had no excuse not to drink and turned her attention back to the Jack Daniels heavy in her hand. The bottle was still nearly full. The dark liquid inside glowed in the dim, green light of the digital clock which now read 3:00 a.m.

They made it to Sam's building, leaving the lights of the city and the Prudential building behind them on Storrow Drive. They managed to stagger up the six flights of stairs to Sam's Allston apartment, on the top floor or the penthouse suite, as he called it.

Outside his door, he held his finger to his lips. "My roommate is probably sleeping," he whispered. For some reason, this struck them both as hilarious and they fought to stifle their laughter.

After a brief struggle with his keys, he got the door open. He grasped her hand and led her in, tiptoeing through the dark apartment and down the hallway to his room. He broke the silence with a sharp, "Dammit" when he stubbed his toe on the door frame. Dayna's hushed giggles triggered more of the same from Sam. He ushered her in and closed the door behind them.

The room was dark until Sam managed to feel his way along the wall to a dresser and switch on a lava lamp. A reddish orange glow flickered across the small room. Dayna chuckled to herself, wondering if he considered it mood lighting.

It looked to her like the room of any college kid. There was a desk, a small bookshelf, a dresser, and a full-sized bed, perhaps a queen. A couple of movie posters were taped to the white walls. Books and pens littered the desk but the room was relatively neat. A pleasant surprise after being in his car.

"Well, this is the mansion," he said. He walked towards her holding the bottle of Jack he must have taken with him from the car. "What do ya think?"

Dayna threw her purse on the dresser and faced him. He smiled, took a big swig, then offered her the bottle. She hesitated. What was she doing with a young guy like him? She accepted his offer and took another swig of whiskey washing down the guilt threatening to surface. She handed the bottle back to him.

The whiskey warmed her, spreading up her neck onto her

cheeks. She imagined the dark liquid clashing with the clear vodka she'd already consumed, a war in her stomach. The room tilted and she stumbled back reaching for the wall but Sam steadied her instead.

"Easy there, ma'am," he said with a butchered southern accent.

She couldn't help but laugh as she clung to his arms for support. *Dammit,* she was really drunk.

"Hey! Ain't nothin' funny 'bout the way I talk," he continued, their laughter unfaltering. He paused. "You are beautiful, you know that?" he said in his normal voice.

Her laughter ceased. She was speechless. Did he really think she was beautiful? She leaned forward and kissed him. To her relief, he didn't pull back, but kissed her harder.

Without breaking their embrace, he pushed her against the wall. A moan escaped her and his kisses became more urgent. She ran her hands down his back as he began to find his way under her dress.

"Wait... wait a minute," she whispered, pushing him away. She couldn't believe she was doing this, sleeping with someone other than her husband. She grabbed the bottle of Jack from the bureau, took another big swig of liquid courage and put it back down. She walked over to the bed, sat down and threw her heels off. "All right," she said.

He stared at her for a moment before approaching. He was nervous and she liked it.

She kissed him on the lips, his cheek and down his neck before taking off his shirt. What she saw was nothing less than expected. The perfect body of youth, rippling with muscle. Running a hand down his chest, she rested it on his belt buckle before they fell onto the bed.

Chapter 9

The next morning, she awoke naked in an unfamiliar bed with, as predicted, a killer headache. Soft snoring emanated from next to her. Rolling onto her side, she looked at Sam who was still in a deep sleep. The grey sheet was pulled down exposing his firm, bare ass. Still unconscious, he turned over onto his back, covering himself with the sheet again as if a sudden breeze had swept through the room.

She studied him, watching the relaxed rise and fall of his chest, tempted to run her fingers over it. Despite being heavily intoxicated, she remembered their sex. She hadn't had sex like that in a long time, especially not with Richard.

Bile rose in her throat. She did not want to think about Richard. He'd betrayed her. She had no loyalty to him anymore. But Sam was so young. What did he say? Twenty-six? She shot up in bed, her heart hammering.

Quietly, she gathered her scattered clothing and dressed. She grabbed her purse from the bureau and opened the door as silently as possible. Shutting it behind her, she could still hear the steady rhythm of Sam's snoring.

She made her way down the unfamiliar hallway until she came upon the bathroom. It was comically small. Poor design placed the sink in front of the door making it nearly impossible to shut while standing. Reluctantly, she left it open.

As she caught sight of the vanity mirror. An image of the black figure skulking in Sam's backseat flashed before her. Every bone in her body was telling her to avoid the mirror, to just leave without a glance, but this was a different circumstance. Last night's slip up with the visor was a drunken mistake—this was a necessity. She couldn't leave Sam's apartment looking like a lunatic with smudged mascara and knots in her hair. Risking her sanity, she took a quick look and was surprised to find her hair in decent shape and makeup relatively intact. She freshened up to the best of her abilities and combed her fingers through her hair.

The pounding in her head was becoming increasingly unpleasant. The mirror opened to a medicine cabinet, so why not help herself?

To her disappointment, it was filled with worthless junk: Listerine, razors, floss. She shut the cabinet discouraged, revealing the eyes of another reflected in the glass. She whirled around to face a young man, standing in checkered boxers with traces of sleep still on his face.

"Hey," he muttered. "I'm Mike, Sam's roommate. Sorry I startled you, just on my way to the bathroom. You must be Mrs. Rivers?"

She stepped out of the bathroom. "Who?" she asked, confused.

"You're Sam's Mom, right? I don't think we've met yet, but it's nice to finally..."

She stopped listening. *Mother?* She lowered her eyes to the floor. That one statement confirmed all her fears. She looked old, like someone's mother. This boy couldn't possibly suspect she had just slept with his roommate. She was definitely no twenty-year-old, anyone could see that. She realized then Sam and Mike would not be reminiscing and high-fiving each other later tonight commemorating his sexual conquest. They would not be commenting on how hot she was. Nor would they be wondering which college she went to and whether they should text her later with or without a damn winky face.

"... Sam's a great guy," he was saying. "It's nice of you to come all the way up here and visit him. Aren't you guys from Kansas or somewhere kind of far?"

He stopped talking. He'd asked a question and was waiting for her to answer like a normal person.

"Mrs. Rivers?" he asked again taking a step forwards.

She pitied him. He was innocent in his assumption. His

foolish question was like asking a fat woman how far along she was. He hadn't meant to hurt her feelings.

Meeting his gaze, she threw him a soft smile. One thick piece of brown hair protruded from the top of his head. She wanted to reach out and fix it, smooth it down with the palm of her hand. But her rage was rising too rapidly, and he was standing too damn close. Her hands shot out with overwhelming force, connecting with his bare, hairless chest. He stumbled back, lost his balance, and fell. The weight of his ass hitting the wooden floor caused a thud, rattling the glasses balanced on the shelf behind him. At the sound, she ran, bolting out into the hall and down the stairs, leaving the echo of the front door slamming and his angry screams behind her.

Chapter 10

Her taxi ride home was silent. Her brain was not, attacking her with a barrage of thoughts. She sat with her head cradled in her hands trying to prevent them from pouring out.

Sam had made her feel beautiful and young, but it was a fleeting feeling, a temporary moment where she'd forgotten her age—and his. Now, as she came down from her high, she felt no better than Richard: captivated by youth, tempted by its lure. Weak.

She dropped her hands and wrapped them around herself. She muttered *stupid* and realized the cab had stopped in front of her house. *Their* house. The house she and Richard had bought and furnished with their generous wedding gifts. The house that twenty-six years later had become her prison.

The newspaper was at the end of the driveway. A thick, black tire track was imprinted on the paper's plastic covering from Richard's Porsche. He never bothered to pick it up before heading to work. It had become yet another one of her many chores. Why would today be any different?

She was still hung over. A sickening pain sat in the front of her head as she stooped for the paper. She brought her hand to her temple, trying to steady herself, resenting the world for spinning. Someone once told her the world always spins, but drunk people are the lucky ones who have the joy of experiencing it.

Once the vertigo subsided, she took a moment to admire her house and its grandiosity, beautiful in the early April morning. She did love the house. Before all this melodrama it had been her sanctuary. She'd raised her child here, kept a little garden, hung a hammock on the back deck. Now, she could no longer ignore the darker side. This beautiful house was the place her husband had cheated, right under her nose, in *their* bed. Although she'd had limited contact with him since then, she couldn't escape signs of his presence: facedown books, reading glasses on a side table, dirty dishes in the sink. He'd become a ghost, an entity sighted occasionally whose presence was inferred from scattered misplaced objects.

The sudden urge to pack her things and flee swept over her. Maybe she'd even leave Richard a note, like in the movies, written hastily on nice stationary in looping cursive; *I'm sorry, it's not you, it's me.*

Screw that! She knew damn well it wasn't her.

Her gaze followed a flowering vine up a trellis to the second floor, where it froze on the far-left window. She squinted, just in case her eyes were playing tricks, but there, in the window of her master bedroom stood a figure. The blurred image retreated from the glass and disappeared into her bedroom. The sun's glare made it difficult to see, but something had been there, the sway of the long curtain panel proved it. Richard was at work— it had to be the dark figure, somehow free from the mirror.

The newspaper slipped from her hand. Dayna inhaled sharply and sprinted from the foot of the driveway to the front door. She barged through the foyer and up the stairs, taking them two at a time. She paused outside the master bedroom. What if she was wrong? What if it was an intruder? Her heart hammered as her mind raced with possible scenarios: an axe-wielding lunatic perched behind the door: a hired assassin with a gun. Deciding to confirm the figure's reality was more important, she swung the door open.

Empty.

She scanned the room for any sign of the phantom. She pushed the door flat against the wall, just to be sure she would not be ambushed from behind and stepped inside. On tiptoe, she tried to see past the bed, then crept over to peek on its far side.

Nothing.

Nothing underneath the bed.

Nothing bulky hiding behind the floor-length, open drapes

where she had glimpsed the shadow from outside.

She moved on to the closets. Using both hands she flung the hanging clothes apart.

Nothing.

She spun in a slow circle. Now she was just pissed. This appearing and disappearing bullshit was driving her insane. She stopped turning, fixing her eyes on the door to the master bath.

She thought about kicking the door in, like a police officer in a raid. Instead, she eased it open and felt for the light switch on the left inside wall, half-expecting someone or something to grab her hand and yank her in. But the illuminated bathroom of imagined horrors yielded nothing.

Her eyes fell on the drawn shower curtain. She advanced towards it, cursing horror movies for associating the innocent shower curtain with homicide. She inhaled, summoned all her courage, and threw open the curtain, wincing at the metallic sound of metal rings sliding against the metal rod.

The tub was empty.

Standing in the bathroom, she was a little disappointed and very confused. What was this thing and what did it want? Without answers, she retraced her steps, shutting the bathroom door, the bedroom door, then wandering back outside to retrieve the paper she'd dropped, sneaking a quick glance back at the empty second-floor window.

Cradling the paper, she shut the front door and set the deadbolt. Where did the real threat lay, outside or inside her own home?

Dayna leaned against the door, exhaled a deep sigh and slid down until she was seated on the floor. Her hangover had worsened from exertion and her head was pounding.

She was positive she'd seen the outline of a figure. It hadn't been some fake phantom from a *Scooby Doo Mystery*, an angry neighbor with a mask who gets exposed by those heroic kids and dog. Maybe she had unintentionally conjured something in that crappy motel and it had attached itself to her; she thought she remembered something like that from a movie. Should she consider contacting a priest to have her home cleansed? Did people even still do that? But there was also another possibility, perhaps the scariest of the three. Maybe the figure wasn't there. Maybe it was all in her head. Maybe she was in fact going crazy.

Chapter 11

Richard found her around 7:00 that night, at the kitchen table, with her head cradled in one hand, a dying cigarette in the other and a glass of whiskey in front of her. The worst part, she didn't even like whiskey.

"Jesus, Dayna," he said, placing his briefcase on the table. "You're smoking again! Are you kidding me? And in the house?" He sounded disgusted. He started to pace, must have thought better of it, and brought his hands to his hips like someone's disappointed mother. "You haven't smoked in years."

She didn't need him to criticize her. She had already scolded herself when she'd rifled through the hutch drawers in search of her old, forgotten pack. She knew smoking was wrong and unhealthy. That's why she had quit all those years ago. She had wanted to be a good example for Max when he was young, not that it worked out: now a secret Marlboro smoker himself.

Glaring at him, she poked the cigarette out, and took the opportunity to light another. It was just so tempting, so easy. Smoking gave her something to do with her hands—and her mind; a mental cleansing of sorts. That's really why people took cigarette breaks; screw the addiction part.

"Unbelievable. What is wrong with you?" he said.

She held her tongue, wishing he would disappear. Maybe a trap door would materialize underneath him, leaving her to thoughts of infidelity and ghosts. Instead, he slapped the cigarette from her hand. It landed on the table and rolled. She lifted her head and looked up at him with resentment.

"You didn't have to do that." It was all she could manage to say; her head was spinning from the dreadful combination of whiskey and nicotine, but at least her hangover had subsided.

"Well, I'm glad to have finally gotten your attention. I thought we were past this... this moping around. We've been doing better."

Dayna picked up the cigarette and took one last drag before extinguishing it in the antique ashtray she'd also dug out from the kitchen hutch. It may have been Richard's mother's. She couldn't remember and didn't care. She reclined in her chair. "We are."

"It doesn't seem like it, does it?" he said, motioning to her. He sighed, his tone softer. "I'm sorry. I just want this to get better. You're my wife and I love you. Don't you think this marriage is worth saving?"

"We don't have a marriage. We have an arrangement," she reminded him, feeling spiteful.

His brow furrowed. "Is that what this is to you? Is that why you didn't come home last night? Monica said you left in a rush. That you knocked wine from Amy's hand. That you didn't seem right."

Bitch.

He took a step forward. "I was worried when you weren't here when I got back. What's going on? Where were you last night?"

"I stopped for a drink. I came home late. Not a big deal."

His eyes narrowed. "Listen, I don't know how many times I need to tell you that I'm sorry, but I'll keep doing it until you believe me. Everyone makes mistakes; nobody's perfect. You need to trust me."

No, it was Richard who needed *her* trust. Memories of the party flooded back, his hands all over that girl, grabbing her ass. "Trust you? Don't be ignorant – it's unattractive," she said, knowing it would hurt him. Standing up, she chugged the rest of her whiskey and set the empty glass on the counter. She turned toward him and crossed her arms.

Richard began to pace. "I get it. You're angry and you have every right to be, but don't push me away. Don't let your anxieties get the better of you. The alcohol and smoking again...

smoking won't give you control—"

"Don't you dare psychoanalyze me, Richard. Don't you fucking dare!" She walked towards him, stopping on the opposite side of the kitchen table. "I'm not one of your clients."

"I'm not trying to. I'm just concerned with these—these violent outbursts you've been having."

"Violent out bursts?" She let out a smug laugh. "This is not a violent outburst, Richard. Or should I call you Dick now?"

He ignored the last comment. "Maybe not this one, but you lit our sheets on fire. Burned them in the fucking tub. What am I supposed to make of that?"

"They were dirty." She mimed a mystified shrug.

He threw his hands up in the air. "You really are unbelievable! It was a one-time thing, I—"

"Wrong! You told me there was another woman before that."

His brow furrowed. He was lying.

Richard cleared his throat. "That's right, but what I meant was—"

"I don't believe you, Richard. You can't even keep the lies straight in your own head." She brought her palm to her forehead. "There's probably been others. I bet you can't keep your hands off any young thing with a pair of tits."

"Dayna, for Christ's sake—"

"Where do you even meet these women? You barely go anywhere outside of work. Are they nurses at McClain's? Other psychiatrists? Clients? Are they—" She stopped. Something she'd said had nicked him. There'd been an instant of panic in his expression. His eyes had widened. A quick inhalation.

"You've really lost it, Dayna," he said and turned away. "I'm not the bad guy here."

She envisioned herself running after him, slapping him across the face and telling him she saw what he did at the party. Calling him a liar, a cheater.

She took a deep breath and started towards the stairs. He

would deny it, just as he had now. He wasn't just lying about the number of affairs, he was hiding something. Something she was sure, he did not want her to find out.

Chapter 12

It was 12:30 a.m. She couldn't sleep. Her thoughts kept returning to their argument, turning Richard's words over in her head. How could he expect her to trust him? He had some nerve to even suggest it. And to say that *she* was losing it… what a laugh! She had witnessed his brief moment of panic: the widening of his eyes, the draw of a quick breath. What had she said again? Anything with a pair of tits. Nurses. Doctors. Clients.

Clients!

Could that really be it? Psychiatrists entering relationships with their clients was a huge ethical violation, in some cases grounds for revoking of medical licenses. If she were to make that accusation, she would need serious proof.

She would search Richard's office. It was the one room in the house off limits to her; not even the cleaning ladies were allowed in there. Richard always claimed someone would mess something up or misplace a file. He had a duty, he'd insisted, to keep client files confidential. She'd never questioned that before, but then again, she never had a reason to.

The clock now read 12:35. The minutes ticked by in excruciating increments. A few hours ago, she'd heard the creak of his footsteps, seen his shadow pass under the door and the hall light switch off. He had to be asleep by now. Richard was an early riser, 5:30 a.m. on workdays.

She sat up in the darkness and swung her legs to the side of the bed, her heart thumping. This might not be the best idea. What if he was still awake?

She glanced at the glowing alarm clock: 12:37. Her feet touched the cold wooden floor. She had to act. The call log Max had helped her dig up revealed nothing. She needed to uncover the secrets, if any, hidden within Richard's office. She was praying for something obvious, perhaps his calendar marked with notes like *cheat on wife tonight at 6:00* that she could shove in his face and say, "See! I knew you couldn't be trusted, you lying sack of shit. I'm leaving!"

On the other hand, maybe she would find nothing. What would she do then? She supposed she could keep an eye on him for a while. If he didn't slip up then maybe, just maybe, they could go back to living their old life: reading in bed together, family dinners, making love. She shivered at the last thought.

She secured her long, black robe around her while trying to slow her pounding heart. She snuck another glance at the alarm clock before easing open the door.

She crept down the hall, cringing at the slightest creaks. On the right, maybe six feet from her room, was Richard's office, another two doors down from that was the guest room he'd been confined to. As she opened the office door, the bottom hinge's tiny scrape sounded deafening. She held her breath and listened. The soft swish of a breeze from the air-condition vent came from above her. But there were no footsteps, no movement. She entered the office and shut the door behind her.

She crept through the darkness towards the back of the room where she switched on an antique desk lamp. It cast a dim light around the room, barely bright enough to see, but it would have to be sufficient.

She thought back to all the times she had poked her head in the office and given Richard a quiet wave. Despite her silence, he would hold one finger to his mouth in a shushing manner, whether dictating into his recorder, rummaging through a mountain of papers or speaking into a phone clamped on his shoulder. Always *shush, not now, I'm busy.*

Richard worked in chaos but left his workspace neat. All that remained on his desk now was a desktop computer, a landline with an ancient answering machine, his outdated electric radio and a crystal battleship paperweight she'd given him for his fiftieth birthday.

Dayna opened the first drawer to a find an organized assortment of pens, tape, paperclips and other various crap. She closed it and moved to the drawer beneath it, which contained a calculator, bank statements and some envelopes. The bottom drawer was double depth, packed tight with manila folders. From the looks of them, they were client files, probably from Richard's private practice in Boston. This was what she was looking for!

Dayna began to skim through them, regarding the names printed in the tab. The files were alphabetized by last name, starting with 'A'.

Adams, Ben... Carter, Thomas... Douglas, Julia...

The names blurred before her eyes. What was she even looking for? Guilt overwhelmed her. All those years of Richard reminding her of confidentiality and here she was reading the names of people who came to her husband for help. *Remember, Dayna, some of these people have very serious problems or issues they perceive as shameful. They do not want their personal information lying around for just anyone to see. Always think of the client.* This was the statement Richard cautioned her with the few times he had discovered a small stack of insurance papers downstairs, on the kitchen table, left unattended. Even if she'd paused for only a few minutes to make a cup of coffee, he acted as if she'd opened the window and thrown their personal information out into the street for everyone to read. *Always think of the client, honey.*

Morris, Henry... McAndrew, Phyliss...

The files appeared to never end, it would take too much time to skim through every one, time she didn't have. She was just about to shut the drawer when she hesitated. A file caught her eye, nestled among the other manilas in the 'M' section—the tab read TATE, JESSICA. It could have been a simple mistake, after all 'M' and 'T' are only separated by a few letters. The only problem, Richard did not make *simple* mistakes like that.

She removed the folder and saw it was covered in little, gold stars. Stars a teacher might give to a good student. She knelt on the floor, her stomach sinking and opened the file. A long, white envelope with her husband's name written in girly cursive with bright, purple pen sat on top of a stack of papers. Her eyes narrowed. What in the world was this? She held the envelope, it felt awkward, like there was something stuffed inside.

Dayna turned it over to find the seal already broken. She reached in and, to her surprise, pulled out a lacey, lilac thong. She dropped it to the floor, disgusted.

Further inspection of the envelope revealed a neatly folded note written in that same girlish cursive as on the front:

You had me thinking about you all night, so I figured I'd give you something to think about until next time. I miss you already.

Jessica.

Her name was surrounded by a big, looping heart. Hands shaking, Dayna stared at the note, tracing the shape of the heart with her eyes. Damn him to hell! Damn them both, for that matter. Why would he keep this paraphernalia as if it was a trophy? Did he come in here at night to hold it in his hands, sniff it and think of this Jessica? And this *girl*—she was clearly infatuated with him, if not in love. Did she know he was married? Did she care?

Dayna refolded the note following its creases and slipped it back into the white envelope. With two fingers, she picked up the thong as if it were hazardous waste and shoved it back in.

She tossed the envelope aside and turned her attention to the assessment packet resting in the folder. Richard gave these assessment packets to all his new clients. The first two pages asked clients to fill out their reason for seeking help, symptoms, medications, family history, and so on. Standard stuff. The last page of the packet contained the client's contact info, address and insurance information.

The packet was filled out in that same girly cursive that'd been scribbled across the envelope. Her eyes skimmed the first page, but found nothing of interest, other than Jessica's age. Twenty-two. How nice.

She tossed the packet aside to reveal a small stack of papers secured with a paper clip. They appeared to be Richard's session notes. She could tell by his horrid handwriting: his mother always joked he was meant to be a doctor with writing like that.

Each page of notes was dated in the right-hand corner. She removed the paper clip and shuffled through them. By the fifth or sixth session, Dayna noticed certain words were underlined: worthlessness, emptiness, unstable. But as the sessions continued the underlined words seemed to apply to erotic themes: fantasies, threesomes, roleplaying. These words were underlined in a deeper manner. Each line had been retraced over and over again, so much so that the paper had worn thin, almost ripping in some spots.

By later sessions, the notes grew thinner, until they stopped altogether: dated blank pages. Dayna swore under her breath. Richard and Jessica had found other ways to fill the hour time slot.

She turned over the last page. Stapled to the back was a Polaroid photo of Jessica. Dayna recognized her from Monica's party, the pretty, blonde girl in a nice dress who had twirled her hair as Richard squeezed her ass. The pretty blonde girl who also had been fucked by Dayna's husband in her bed. However, in this photo Jessica wasn't wearing a dress. She sat topless in a leather chair Dayna recognized from Richard's office in Boston. She was in a thong with her legs crossed. Her hands covered her nipples and pushed her breasts together, making them appear more voluptuous than they really were, although Dayna remembered them being substantial enough. A flirtatious smile was spread across her face, her eyes soft. Dayna held it at arm's length: nice photo if not for the goddamn circumstances.

Dayna's heart quickened and ached from betrayal. She wanted to tear the photo into shreds and hurl the notes around the office. But this was the proof she needed of long-term infidelity—and with a client. Richard couldn't claim a one-time moment of weakness. The sick bastard had kept trophies, for God's sake! Picture. Underwear. Love note.

She re-secured the session notes with trembling hands and placed them and the assessment packet back into the folder and closed it. She looked at the tab again, committing the name to memory: TATE, JESSICA. Next to that were the letters BPD.

She skimmed through the rest of the folders in the 'M' section, searching for any out of place. Her fingers skated over the tabs. She made it through ten before they halted on another folder marked with the same little, gold stars. The name read WILSON, AUDREY-BPD. Dayna removed the folder and disassembled its insides. To her dismay, she found similar underlined notes complete with a matching Polaroid. This one depicted a girl she presumed to be Audrey, in a lacey bra and underwear. Smiling, she was posed like a pinup girl, draped across the same brown leather chair.

Her heart escalated from a steady thump to pounding. Dropping Audrey's folder, Dayna turned her attention back to the manilas. Resuming her investigation, she uncovered three more folders, each marked with teacher's gold stars and the same three letters BPD. All contained strange notes complete with a Polaroid of each girl. One was brunette, another blonde, the last a red head. The only thing they all had in common — they were all under the age of twenty-five. She had gathered that from their intake packets.

Dayna reassembled each folder and, to the best of her ability, placed them back where she'd found them. She wouldn't take them tonight. No. She needed time to think. Maybe she'd check his cell records again, research local divorce lawyers. Somehow, part of her was still in denial. This man couldn't be her husband. *Her* husband would never do this.

She closed the drawer, but remained on the floor, unsure if she could stand. A deep pit formed in her stomach. Those little gold stars gave her an unsettling feeling. But the photos devastated her. And BPD—what did those three letters mean? The only word that came to her head was blood pressure, but that couldn't be it.

While on the floor she came to another slow boil. Richard had been cheating on her for over ten years with five different women. From what she'd gathered, each affair lasted about two years, a few even overlapping. How disgusting that Richard was fucking other women, then coming home and making love to her, pretending she was the only one.

And worse: he'd chosen to have affairs with girls less than half his age. Maybe it would've hurt less if he'd chosen a successful, middle-aged business woman. Maybe...

"What are you doing in here?" Richard asked from behind her.

A small scream leapt from her throat. "Jesus, you scared me."

"What are you doing in here?" he asked again.

"I... I heard a noise. I came to see what it was."

He raised an eyebrow.

"And I dropped my ring." She brought her hands in between her legs and slid her wedding ring from her finger, hands shaking. She pretended to feel around on the rug for a few seconds before holding it up to him. "Since I lost some more weight, the thing has been so damn loose."

"I'm glad you found it. We wouldn't want you losing that."

"No. We wouldn't."

His eyes narrowed. "Is something wrong?"

"What?"

"Is something wrong?"

She swallowed hard. It tasted of fear and shame, like she'd been caught masturbating. "No. No. Of course not. Why would there be?"

"It's just that if you heard a noise I thought you might be scared. Maybe let your little mind wander, thinking it was a burglar or a madman... maybe even a ghost?"

"No. I'm fine, really." Dayna shoved herself to her feet, her knees aching. How much had he seen?

"Good. Now why don't you come on out of there and get back to bed."

He reached out a hand that she took with reluctance. He gripped it as if he suspected she might try to run. He led her into the hall, making a point of shutting the office door behind him. Dropping her hand, he kissed her on the forehead.

"Goodnight, honey. Sweet dreams."

That night she dreamt she was in Richard's office. Jessica sat on the brown leather chair's matching love seat, where Audrey lay with her head in her lap, each in a lacy bra and underwear set: Jessica's turquoise, Audrey's lilac. Richard stood behind his desk, muttering nonsensical words to himself.

Dayna moved forward, apparently invisible. As she inched closer to Richard, she saw his eyes were pure black, the whites completely gone.

He advanced towards the girls, concealing something behind his back, like a parent hiding a new toy from their child on Christmas morning. Dayna turned towards them and saw that Jessica was rubbing Audrey's head, whispering to her as if she was cooing to a baby.

Richard removed a drill from behind his back, the silver of the corkscrew gleaming. She watched as he held the drill to Audrey's skull.

Oh God! Dayna's stomach turned over and she screamed, trying to warn Audrey, but no sound came out.

Jessica's cooing was drowned out by the roaring of the drill as it plunged into the soft flesh of Audrey's head. A fountain of blood and chunks of scalp flew into the air.

Dayna woke up on her back, sweating, panting, heart pounding. The black figure stood above her bed. She blinked, and it was gone.

Chapter 13

Despite four hours of sleep, she was at the gym and on the elliptical by 9:00 a.m. She ran in a fury for thirty-minutes. Away went almost three hundred calories, but not her rage.

She pressed the cool down button and walked for two minutes, her body drenched in a thick, angry sweat.

She stared at the TV mounted on the wall but couldn't focus on the content. *BPD*. What the hell did that mean?

She hopped off the elliptical, grabbed her water bottle, and headed for the car. No locker room. No showering. Too many mirrors.

She was almost to her car when she heard, "Dayna?"

Connie was waving from the side of her black Suburban. She must have just arrived. Her friend looked cool as a cucumber. Her too blonde hair was pulled back into a tight ponytail, each strand superglued in place and her dangling curls could have been a high school cheerleader's. An hour from now, Connie would probably leave looking as she arrived. A hard workout for Connie was sitting on the stationary bike with a Cosmo magazine and smoothie.

"Hey," Dayna said, throwing her a smile.

Stuffed into black workout pants with hot pink stripes running down the legs and her matching sports bra peeking from beneath her sweatshirt, Connie ambled toward her. "How have you been, sweetheart?"

Dayna wondered what her real question was. "Other than the sweat," she said, "I'm good. How about—"

"I'm good. It's just—I just was worried after you left Monica's in such a rush. All the girls were." She paused, her face twisting in concern. "Is everything okay?"

There it was, what she really wanted to know. "Yeah, everything's great."

Connie raised an eyebrow.

Dayna shrugged. "You know, just a little too much to drink, that's all."

"Uh-huh. Well, we were worried about you," Connie said. "I was worried about you."

"No, really," Dayna said. She glanced at her watch, then at her car. "I'm okay."

Connie wilted. "I won't keep you." She took a quick step forward and put a hand on Dayna's forearm. "But if you ever need anything, anything at all, know that I'm here for you."

It was a cliché thing to say, but for some strange reason it meant something coming from Connie. She was a vivacious woman who sometimes teetered on the edge of obnoxiousness, but her intentions were good. Softening, Dayna said, "We could do lunch sometime? Just us?"

"I'd love that," Connie gushed.

"Great."

"And I'll see you at the fundraiser tonight."

Dayna cursed inside: the dreaded fundraiser, every year on the first of May. Richard had been leaving sticky notes on the kitchen table all week. "Wouldn't miss it," she said with her best mock enthusiasm.

Connie smiled, and Dayna raised a hand in farewell. She was halfway to her car when the thought hit her. She stopped and turned. "Do you know what BPD means by chance?"

But Connie had already disappeared into the gym.

Wellesley's Riverway Country Club was this year's host for the *Another Way* fundraiser. The money would be sent to Massachusetts's suicide prevention hotlines and used to increase suicide awareness. It was a good cause, but Dayna had always thought the name *Another Way* sounded condescending, like they were trying to enlighten folks with the light of the Lord.

The twenty-minute car ride to the club was an exercise in

keeping silent. Dayna sat looking out the passenger window, ignoring Richard's weak attempts to start a conversation. Initially, she had considered backing out, claiming an upset stomach or headache, but figured that would be too obvious. She couldn't have Richard suspecting she'd found his little stash of perverted trophies.

"Nice day today. It's finally starting to warm up," Richard said.

She ignored his desperate attempt at mindless chatter.

He cleared his throat. "Thanks for coming with me by the way. I know you had a bit of a late night."

She caught his sideways glance in her peripheral vision. Her cheeks flushed with anger. Why were they stuck in this horrible cycle? She was sick of pretending things were fine while Richard's little jabs and passive aggressive remarks hinted things were far from it. She sighed. "The fundraiser is important to me, too. I'm not doing this for you. I'm doing it because it's right."

She hadn't said much, but it was enough to shut Richard up for the rest of the drive.

As they pulled into the long driveway of The Riverway, the white building loomed over them. Columns lined the front, supporting the overhanging roof and the grand, stone stairs up to the main doors were something out of *Gone With The Wind*. It reminded her of a rich, white man's plantation house. A century ago, fields of cotton could have surrounded the place; today, it centered a golf course.

As the car came to rest, a young man with shirt, tie, and nice biceps opened her door. "Ma'am," he said, offering his hand.

Before a valet had reached Richard's door, he threw it open, dashed around the front of the car and elbowed Dayna's escort out of the way. He gripped her hand, draped it over his arm, and led her up the stairs.

"Keys are in her," he called over his shoulder.

Dayna allowed him his little pretense, but just barely.

Dayna accompanied Richard to the first of the club's three function rooms, her hand still grasped in a not so welcome embrace. Inside, the low, blurred hum of conversation greeted them. A hundred or so people filled the room. To the left, a dozen were gathered around a food table. Another dozen, mostly men, were waiting in line, two abreast, at the cash bar. Dayna glimpsed Monica in the room's center. At almost six-one, she was hard to miss, towering over Greg. Connie was at her side in a black sequin dress. Her hair still piled high in those same cheerleader curls she had sported earlier at the gym.

The sight of Monica caused Dayna's stomach to turn to mush. After her premature flight at Monica's party, Dayna expected a grilling. She hoped that Connie had filled her in on their conversation earlier and had warned Monica that she had just had too much wine, nothing worth mentioning. Before she could get her nerves under control, Richard set off toward them, dragging Dayna behind. She upped the pace to appear his equal, instead of a child being towed to the dentist's office by a parent.

She managed to shake off Richard's hand before they reached her group of friends. Richard, of course, hailed everyone with no hint that anything was wrong, and to her relief, Monica and Connie greeted her with a kiss and no mention of her premature exit. She had just begun to relax when a firm hand landed on her left shoulder.

"There's my favorite couple."

She winced at the statement and turned to find Mark behind her. He inserted himself between her and Richard, with one hand on each of their shoulders. "No offense," he added, nodding towards Greg and Monica.

"Yeah, none taken, you dirt bag," Greg joked. "Can you believe this guy? A jerk to me on my own night," he said to Monica, laughing.

"Hey, buddy, long time no see." Richard shook Mark's hand and flashed one of his bright smiles.

Dayna had to admit her husband could be charming when he wasn't being a pervert.

"You're telling me. You got to get back into golf. We would see much more of each other," Mark said with a mischievous smile, then angled towards her. "My dear, Dayna, looking beautiful as always." He planted a wet kiss on her cheek.

She fought the urge to wipe it away and forced a smile. "Good to see you, Mark."

Mark had always reminded her of an older version of her husband. They were both workaholics who enjoyed whiskey and were too charismatic for their own good. About ten years older than Richard, Mark was a mentor to her husband and father figure. He was a big shot in the psychiatry field and once a professor at Boston University where he first met Greg and Richard. Her husband had worked as a research assistant under him throughout his schooling. Mark gave Richard his first job at his private practice, where he worked for almost six years before starting his own. Now, edging close to retirement, Mark had stopped seeing patients and focused on research, publishing and fundraising for suicide awareness and prevention. Twenty years ago, he had treated Greg's sister, Marlene, for what, Dayna wasn't sure. According to Richard, Greg had found Marlene in her apartment with an empty bottle of vodka by her side and a plastic bag on her head. Apparently, the Beatle's *Eleanor Rigby* had been playing when he found her. Since then, hearing the song always gave Dayna the jitters.

Mark's wife, Marilyn, was standing two steps behind him with a blank face. Her hands were clasped in front of her slender waist, as if playing the role of a dutiful wife, accustomed to being excluded from her husband's dealings. Her long, platinum grey hair was twisted into a neat updo. Dayna had known Mark for over twenty years, but had only met Marilyn a handful of times, usually at these fundraising events. Dayna knew very little about her other than her love of cats and that she was from

Texas. Or was it Florida?

Dayna stepped past Mark to say hello. Marilyn returned her hug as if in a trance.

"Good to see you," Dayna said. "Glad we could make it."

"Me too," Marilyn said in a weak voice, her eyes averted.

Dayna stood for a moment in awkward silence until Monica and Connie made their way from the other side of the huddle to hers.

"Let's find our seats," Monica said. "I think we are all sitting together."

The four women were seated at a table by the stage, VIP seating Dayna guessed, judging by the place setting markers. When the waiter came around, each ordered a glass of white wine. Dayna had fantasized about ordering a martini, but with reluctance, conformed to the other women's choices.

"Sometimes those men of ours can be so boring," Monica said, raising her glass the instant it arrived. "Anyway, how are your cats, Marilyn? Mark said something about surgery?"

"Surgery?" Connie echoed.

How are your cats? Dayna kept a straight face. Was this what life had come to, inquiring about this woman's cats?

Marilyn answered, "Well, Twitch is feeling much better now. Just a broken paw. Must've done it jumping off the back fence. I told Mark that it was too high, but he..."

Monica and Connie were both nodding their heads in sympathy at the earth-shattering importance of the information. Dayna's head felt foggy. She tried concentrating on the square place marker centered behind her plate: RESERVED FOR MRS. DAYNA HARRIS. Then eyed the place marker to her left which indicated her husband's designated spot. At any moment Richard would arrive and plop in the empty seat beside her. Could she really handle that right now? His fake happiness. His witty remarks. The chance he would reach out and take her hand. Why was she even at this function with a man she hated, pretending to be happy? Her marriage was disintegrating and here she was talking about cats. Reality was hitting, and it was hitting hard. She had to leave!

She reached for her pack of Marlboros hidden within her purse and jumped up, her thighs bumping the table on the way up. "I'm going out for a cigarette," she blurted and headed for the closest exit sign, feeling the women's judgmental stares burning into her back. Halfway to the door, she hesitated. She'd left her phone on the table. What the hell? Get it later, and let Marilyn have her shining moment.

Chapter 14

The sun had just begun to set and the air felt cool and crisp against her skin. Dayna was glad she'd chosen to wear her long-sleeved, knee-length, black dress for an unpredictable New England April evening.

She lit a cigarette as she strode to the walking trail she had discover behind the club last year after stepping out for some fresh air in between auctions.

A dirt path with patches of pavement, as if construction workers just gave up, paralleled a narrow stream no more than six feet wide. It was just enough of a preserved area to give city people the illusion of nature and isolation, which was exactly what she needed right now. There wasn't enough booze in the world to help her sit through the rest of the function. God help them all when Mark's long, rambling speech began.

The soft sound of the stream had a calming effect, allowing Dayna to clear her head. Her cigarette was burning low. She would have to return to the fundraiser soon and was trying to decide the best and least obtrusive way to do so.

She'd almost finished another cigarette before noticing how quickly the day had given way to twilight. Darkness could be funny like that, gradually sneaking up on you. But the darkness in Wellesley was nothing like the darkness in the country. Her uncle had lived in a small New Hampshire town where light was limited after sunset and streetlights nonexistent. Her family visited often, and it was there she'd learned what real darkness was. Real darkness caused you to turn your head and check behind you, unsure who or what might be following. And although this darkness was nothing like the one she remembered from her childhood, it sent a chill down her spine all the same.

With night creeping in, Dayna favored the side of the path closest to the scattered lampposts. She recalled a small bridge up ahead; she would walk to that before heading back. She shivered and wrapped her arms around her for warmth. The temperature seemed to have dropped ten degrees in the last few minutes.

Taking one last drag from her cigarette, she tossed it to the ground and stamped it out. Her heel made a crunching sound against the sparse gravel. She glanced down to ensure the ember was extinguished and noticed a crow. It was dead, wings by its side, only a few inches from her foot. She gasped and jumped back. Poor guy must've fallen out of his nest and broken his neck.

She skirted the carcass and, two steps later, spotted another dead bird and beyond that, several more. With each discovery, an unsettling horror built. Dayna halted, looking ahead. Dead birds were scattered down the path. Forty crows, maybe more. There was no way to proceed without stepping on them and crunching their little bones.

Something flickered ahead, a moving shadow underneath one of the lampposts. Her body grew cold all over. Thirty feet ahead, beyond the carpet of birds, stood the figure. Her stomach cringed.

For a moment Dayna stood still, paralyzed, afraid to move. The figure stared back at her. Dayna mustered enough courage to take a step back, then whipped around to flee in the direction of the club. After turning a corner in the trail, she slowed, then stopped and listened: nothing. Not a creak of branches, not the chirp of crickets, not a rustle of footsteps on dead leaves. From ahead came a tinkle of music, a faint bumping of bass, and hint of conversation emanating from the club. She continued, forcing herself to maintain a sane pace, despite her uncanny feeling that *it* was following her.

She rounded a bend and stopped dead. Ahead of her stood the figure.

Dayna's heart lurched and dizziness overcame her. The bright lights from the club's patio beckoned in the distance, but she was trapped. She wheeled around, retracing her steps.

The breaking of sticks and rustling of leaves began behind her. Dayna picked up the pace, her pulse drumming in her ears. Up ahead she saw the bridge. She was right back to where she'd first seen the figure, on the trail covered with dead crows. Tears materialized in her eyes. She stopped. Enough of this tormenting and fear.

"What do you want from me?" she screamed. The rustling halted. "What do you want?" she asked again, her voice sounding shrill even to her own ears.

She spun in a slow circle, catching sight of the figure in the stream. Determined, she marched towards it. "What do you want?" she yelled again.

Perhaps she should confront this thing straight on; deal with it. She advanced a step and paused. The figure's stillness punctured her confidence and any bit of courage seeped from her like blood from an open wound.

"Leave me alone. Please, just leave me alone." She sounded like a hopeless little girl and hated herself for it.

The figure trod through the water towards the dark underside of the bridge. As it edged closer to the darkness, an unexpected desperation swelled in her, propelling her forward into the stream. The coldness of the water hit her feet, then her calves, then her thighs. Her heels seeped into the sand, fighting her with every step, but she trudged on. The figure stopped and turned to face her, beckoning her forward with a dead, grey hand.

"What do you want?" she asked.

The figure did not respond. It motioned her forward and Dayna continued. With each step her heels sank deeper into the muddy bottom, until she lost her footing and fell forwards into the dark, murky water. She clenched her eyes shut, felt around, and dug her heels back in to the stream's bottom. She shot up, a gasp escaping her. Her dress was soaked through, her heels filled with mud.

Her eyes locked back onto the figure's. She was angry and

cold. "Is this what you want? To ruin my life?" She paused, waiting for an answer she knew would never come. "Well, just go ahead! Do it!" Despite the cold her cheeks felt hot with anger. She brought her hands to her face. A desperate cry was forming, but she sucked it back in and dropped her hands. She stared into the grey eyes that peered from underneath the hood. "Please. I'll do whatever you want."

As soon as the words left her lips, the figure melted into the stream, transforming into a dark, inky blackness. Dayna stood, horrified. Was it coming for her? She pictured it slinking through the water like a crocodile. She turned, wanting to bolt from the stream, but her heels caused her to stumble. She managed to steady herself before tottering face first again. Her heart raced, and she searched the water for movement.

She heard a new sound, the distant giggle of a girl. The crunching of dead leaves and the voices of young men followed. Four teenagers came into view beneath the nearest lamp post, two girls and two boys. She heard the clinking of bottles, saw the orange flick of a lighter and smelled the potent, unmistakable scent of marijuana. Their hushed giggles and murmured talk came to an abrupt stop as one of the boys caught sight of her in the steam. He pointed to her, their voices fell quiet.

"Hey! Do you need help?" the boy who first spotted her asked.

She flinched at the sound of his voice.

"Hey, lady?" he called again. He glanced back to his friends.

Dayna shook her head.

"Whatever," he finally said. He threw up a hand in a dramatic fashion, then took a long swig of his beer before sauntering away. His posse followed.

"What a fucking psycho," the other boy muttered, eliciting giggles from the girls.

"Seriously," the first boy responded.

They continued down the path, all of them laughing. The

breaking of a beer bottle caused her to jump.

"Don't drown," one of the girls called back in a mocking voice.

"Maybe she's crazy," someone said.

Maybe she was.

Shivering, Dayna stood until she could no longer hear their crunching footsteps and hurtful laughter. She took some satisfaction in knowing those kids had to make their way through all those crows. She pictured the girls squealing and crying, asking to be picked up by the boys who would struggle to carry their weight, as scared by the dead birds as she'd been — but never admitting it.

It wasn't until she was wading back towards shore that she realized she hadn't heard any mention of the crows. How could that be? Those fucking birds were everywhere.

Dayna struggled to gain her footing on land but managed to pull herself up using a tree root. She hobbled towards the trail. She looked down the path in the direction the teenagers had travelled.

There were no crows at all, not a single one.

Chapter 15

Dayna was exhausted, confused and soaking wet. Droplets of water fell from her hair into her eyes, blurring her vision. The water had been cold to begin with and the crisp air blowing against her wet skin left her shivering.

When the trail forked, she chose the path spitting her out onto the main road. She did not want to go anywhere near the club. God forbid someone see her like this.

She spotted an intersection and uttered a sigh of relief. The woods had made her paranoid, the trees becoming phantoms, the wind ghostly fingers on her neck.

It was late enough that few people were out, and they were mostly drunks. Even so, she still suffered a few stares of disgust and even fear. Then again, they'd probably think any woman running through the streets of Wellesley, soaking wet with wild eyes, must not be too right in the head. Maybe even dangerous.

She paused at the corner with one arm wrapped around her abdomen for warmth, the other raised to hail a taxi. Four empty cabs drove by before one stopped. The cabbie looked her over and stared through the rearview mirror as she slid into the plastic-covered seat. This was what it must feel like to be a crazy person. Even after giving her address, he kept eyeing her.

"What?" she snapped.

He shook his head, as if coming out of a trance, and accelerated. He continued to sneak occasional glances, maybe afraid she would try to knife and rob him. Dayna leaned her head against the window as a tear rolled down her face.

It was a long, uncomfortable taxi ride, made even more embarrassing when she arrived home. After explaining she had no money and would have to run inside to grab some, the cabbie yelled at her in a thick, Jamaican accent.

"Jesus!" she said, slamming the door. "I said I'd be right

back." Everyone nowadays was so goddamn selfish. She could have been brutally beaten, raped and left for dead and all this man cared about was his fifteen bucks.

When she returned, she threw it through the open window, waiting to see the look on his face.

"Are you fucking crazy?" he called out the window.

She gave him the finger.

Upstairs, Dayna fought her way out of her damp dress, the resisting fabric clinging to her like masking tape. She was soaked through; everything would have to be changed.

She wanted to shower, but was too afraid Richard would return home and catch her off guard. She settled for putting on fresh underwear and her favorite silk nightdress. Its soothing coolness was a welcome relief against her tired body.

As she ran a brush through her damp and tangled hair, headlights illuminated the room. She glanced out the window to see Richard's white Porsche pulling into the driveway. She reached for her black robe and tied it around her as if fastening battle armor.

A few moments later, she heard the slamming of the downstairs door, followed by an angry shout.

"Dayna? Dayna, are you here?"

It reminded her of her father when he would come home drunk, waking the whole house with his thunderous yelling.

"You left me there again. Alone. Two fucking nights in a row. Do you know what that makes me look like?" He paused, and she waited for the answer. "A fool. A fucking fool. I ran around for twenty minutes looking for you, asking politely if anyone had seen my dear, sweet wife. No one had. Do you know how embarrassing it was to leave without you? To just leave and hope you were here?"

"Well, I'm here," she called. "Oh, and by the way, I'm fine. Safe and sound, thanks for asking."

His footsteps sounded on the stairs. "Get out here!" he bellowed. "We are going to have to have a serious discussion about this right now."

She hesitated, irritated by his demand and the entitlement she detected in his voice. But she'd have to let him get it off his chest eventually. She made her way to the landing, bracing herself for his fury. Richard stood halfway up the stairs with one hand on the railing, the other on his hip, his face bright red.

"What?" He glared at her. "You took a shower? You left me there to come home and take a fucking shower?"

She flinched at the word *fucking*. Richard wasn't usually one for swearing, but the past few days he couldn't seem to get enough of it.

"I had too much to drink," she responded. Her go-to lie.

"Too much to drink? Of course. Not only is my marriage disintegrating, but my wife has become an alcoholic. I'm not going to pretend I don't see those bottles of wine disappear from the fridge."

Rage overcame her. "Don't you dare patronize me and act like I'm the problem. You're the liar, Richard. You've been lying to me for ten years." She was taken aback by her own boldness, but it felt good.

His lips parted, eyes narrowing. It was the face he made when he wanted to interrupt her.

She steamrolled on. "And to think all this time it was sitting right under my nose." She snorted a laugh. "You probably never would have even gotten caught if you hadn't brought that girl into *our* bed. What, it wasn't exciting enough for you? You had to fuck her where we sleep. Did that really get you off?"

"Dayna..."

"I was going to wait to tell you, but I know about the others, too."

He blinked, straightening as if slapped. "What are you talking about? There weren't—"

"It wasn't just Jessica. I saw the files."

"Where?"

"Your desk drawer."

"What are you talking about?"

"Oh, don't do that. You know exactly what I'm talking about."

The red of his face brightened. "You bitch!" He lunged up the stairs. Gripping her forearm and dragged her down the hallway towards the office.

"Richard!" she yelled, gasping in pain.

He threw open the door, pulled her inside and spun her around. "Stay there," he shouted. He ran over to his desk and started yanking open drawers.

"See?" He motioned to her. "I've got nothing to hide."

She stood, motionless.

"Look, dammit," he said, pointing.

She moved towards the desk, looking to him for confirmation before scanning through the folders in the lower drawer. They weren't there. No folders marked with little golden stars. No envelope shoved in back. No evidence of any Jessica Tate.

"I…" she stammered, skimming through the folders again. Her hands were shaking. She pulled open the other two drawers just to make sure he hadn't hidden them, but there was no sign of them.

"I don't know what you think you saw, but there's nothing here."

"I don't… I mean…" Fearing that she was on to him, he must have gotten to them first.

"You're not well, honey. You're seeing things. I don't know, maybe the alcohol is the problem here. I think it's causing your insecurities to get the better of you. Obsessing about my infidelity has only caused you to imagine it to be true. Not to mention, delirium can be a symptom of alcohol abuse. Did you know that?"

Was he right? Now, she was doubting her own sanity, unsure

if she could be trusted. Had the folders ever really been there? Of course they had. She could remember feeling them. They'd been rough on her finger tips as she'd skimmed through them. Richard was trying to confuse her. Manipulate her.

"I know what I saw."

"I understand you think you saw something incriminating in my, what did you say? My desk drawer? But I'm afraid you're mistaken, honey. Isn't that obvious?" He said it like it was the saddest thing he'd ever said, like the family dog had just been hit by a car and he was trying to explain it to a child.

He reached out to take her hand. She jerked away and ran out of the office and down the hall to his bedroom. Starting with the dresser, she pulled out each drawer, dumping socks, underwear, and tee-shirts on the floor.

"Dayna. Dayna!"

"Liar," she shouted back at him. Moving to the closet, she rose on the balls of her feet to feel along the top shelf. To her disappointment, there were no stacks of files, no cardboard boxes, no bin or safe of any kind.

She pressed the pillowcases, then ducked down to peer under the bed. "Where are they?" she yelled.

Richard stood in the doorway, arms folded, a smug expression on his face. "Dayna, please. This is ridiculous."

"Where?" She grabbed a book from the bedside table and chucked it at him, then his phone charger.

Richard shielded his face and advanced towards her. She was near hysterics and tearing at the bed sheets, ripping them from the bed. He grabbed her arms to restrain her.

"Where?" she repeated, succumbing to tears, ashamed she was crying in front of him.

"Honey, I don't know what you're talking about." He shushed her like a crying baby, trying to pat her back. It reminded her of her dream. Jessica cooing Audrey on the leather love seat just before Richard plunged the drill into her skull.

"Liar." She wriggled from his grip. "Fucking liar."

He tried to reach out, take ahold of her again, but she pushed him away.

"Don't you touch me."

She dashed from the room and down the hall to her own bedroom. She slammed the door and stood with her back against it. Breathing hard, she waited for Richard to come after her, but heard nothing.

A glimmer of grim satisfaction peeked through her despair. At least she'd made a mess of his room. He'd have to remake his bed and restock his drawers. He'd probably be muttering, cursing her under his breath. Served him right.

This was how marriages ended, wasn't it? With confusion and lies?

She trudged to the bed, lay down and stared at the ceiling. The happy times, the scrapbook-worthy moments, all seemed so surreal. So distant.

Chapter 16

Dayna spent most of the next day lying in bed. At one point, she moved into the living room, a blanket wrapped around her, and turned on the television. *Intervention* was playing, but she didn't want to watch it. It was no longer entertaining to watch drug addicts and alcoholics ruin their lives and destroy their families. Instead, she stared past the TV at the wall, barely blinking.

She sat until the sun faded and darkness filled the room. Where to go from here? When people get married they think it's for the long haul. No one gets married with the intention of things going bad. Nobody dreams of having two or three marriages and an ugly divorce. What would she do if she left Richard? Where would she go? Would she date again? She sure as hell wasn't ready to retire to a life of cats and crossword puzzles. But she was older now, almost fifty. She had no job, not since she'd "quit" her position as Richard's secretary. She supposed she could go back to working at the bank. Maybe take a few classes to catch up on the changing technology.

Why was this decision so hard? She had every right to leave Richard. What he did was wrong, not to mention unethical. Dating clients was a no, no. Career suicide. He could lose his license—and he knew it. That's why he got rid of the evidence. He feared she would use it against him, tarnish his reputation out of anger and vengeance. Maybe she would have. All these years he'd kept evidence, called these girls from his private cell phone and fucked them in her bed. He was cocky. Blinded by confidence. He reminded her of a serial killer who was so sure he'd never get caught that he ended up making the simplest of mistakes. He probably got off by hiding it from her.

She hated him.

She jumped when her phone buzzed. She'd left it on the end table in case Max called. She hadn't heard from him in a few days. With her eyes acclimated to the darkness, the phone's light was blinding and she had to squint to make out the name, 'Connie'. She opened the text message.

Hi, Dayna. I know we agreed to lunch the other day, but how about dinner? The hubby's out of town. Say 7:00 at Brookline Grille?

The clock read 6:30. Connie wasn't asking as much as she was telling her. Dayna wanted to say no, tell her it wasn't a good time. Deep down, though, she knew going would be good for her. Plus, Richard would be home around 7:00 and she did not want to be here when he returned.

She responded with a *'See you then'*.

Being in no mood to drive up and down Beacon street searching for parking, Dayna took a cab to the restaurant.

She spotted Connie at a window table, staring into an iPhone armored in a hot-pink case. "Sorry I kept you waiting," Dayna said, sliding into the booth across from her.

Connie raised her head, breaking into a huge grin. "Hi, honey! It's no problem. I have my brain sucker," she said, jingling her phone. "The constant access to email and Facebook is turning us into a bunch of mouth breathers, don't ya think?" Connie's grin widened as she slipped her phone back into her Michael Khor's bag. Her nails and lipstick matched the iPhone case.

The waitress approached, a young girl with short black hair, who introduced herself as Kristen. She was a pretty little thing and Dayna wondered if she was Richard's type.

Connie ordered them two glasses of Chardonnay and herself a Caesar salad wrap with shrimp, no fries, proclaiming she had to watch her calories. Dayna ordered the same, minus the shrimp, but kept the fries. Who gives a shit about calories when your husband has already traded you in for the new model?

Kristen smiled and wheeled around, folding up her unused notepad. Dayna's eyes followed her. An image of Kristen in lingerie bending over Richard's brown leather chair popped into her mind.

"Everything okay?" Connie asked.

Dayna nodded, the image fading.

Connie seemed skeptical but appeared to brush it off. "So... I was delighted when you suggested we do lunch or well, dinner I suppose. We hardly ever have you and me time. You know? When it's just the two of us, no Monica." Connie paused. "Plus, this place has the best wraps," she said, chuckling.

Kristen was back and set down two wine glasses. Connie's bangle bracelets clanged like wind chimes as she reached for hers.

"Pretty," Dayna remarked.

"Thanks. Doug picked these up for me in Italy."

Doug was Connie's husband. His work as an event planner took him all around the country and sometimes overseas.

"So, how's the family?"

Connie asked it with so much enthusiasm, Dayna was afraid to answer. She was tempted to lie, as terrified to confide in Connie as she had anticipated. She slid the wineglass toward her, staring at the reflections of the overhead lights on the surface. "I—well, that's actually what I wanted to talk to you about." She took a deep breath. "Richard and I are having some problems."

She was surprised by the immediate sense of relief that washed over her. She had been keeping it to herself for so long it felt good to say it aloud instead of falling over herself trying to cover up.

Connie's brow furrowed. "Bedroom problems?"

The heat of a blush spread across Dayna's cheeks. "I guess you could call it that. Richard was—is having an affair."

Connie's mouth dropped. "Oh, honey. Jesus. How did you find out? When did this happen?"

"I don't know, maybe four weeks ago. I walked in on them." She paused. "In our bed."

"Well, fucking hell. What an animal."

"What's worse, this girl is maybe twenty-two. Can you believe that? I just—"

"Twenty-two?" Connie whistled, imitating the sound of a missile coming into landing. "Jesus Christ! What an asshole," she said, shaking her head. "You know what my mother always said: men are like sharks and once they get a taste of that young blood, they always come back for more."

Finally, some positive feedback, just what she needed. Someone to tell her Richard was an asshole, a piece of shit. Someone to remind her she wasn't the crazy one. "He said he ended it, that it was a mistake. But I know he's still seeing her. I saw them together at Monica's party."

Connie nodded. "Now it makes sense why you left. She was at the party? Who is this girl?"

"She was one of his clients, at least that's what I think. I don't know much else." Dayna left it at that, keeping the folders, the pictures and the other girls to herself. The rest was too embarrassing, too perverted.

"A client?" Connie said. "That's a big no, no. I know it happens, like all these high school teachers dating students and getting them pregnant, but it's not right. It's unethical."

"You're telling me." Dayna sampled her wine, trying to fight the tears threatening to form.

"Are you going to file papers?" Connie asked.

Before she could answer, Kristen returned and placed their wraps in front of them. Dayna fantasized about grabbing her by her pretty, heart-shaped pendant and screaming at her to never get married. To never become a lady talking of affairs and divorce over Caesar salad wraps, worrying a young waitress might overhear. Instead, she thanked her and waited for her to walk away.

"I don't know. I mean… at first, I was sure of it. I was going to be done, move out. The whole enchilada. But it's hard. I mean, outside of Richard's office, I haven't worked in over ten years.

Not to mention I'm almost fifty. It's a lot harder to start over. I just don't know what to do anymore."

Connie reached out and placed a soft hand on top of Dayna's. "I understand. I sure as hell wouldn't want to be starting over at this age. I'll be fifty-five come July. Can you believe that? You're a spring chicken compared to me." She laughed, and Dayna found herself laughing too. They stopped and sipped their wine. "Well, if you ever change your mind, let me know. One of Doug's close friends is a divorce lawyer and he's *very* good at what he does."

Dayna nodded. "It's just funny," she began. "Women our age are supposed to be the wise ones, the ones who have it all together. And here I am holding on to this man after everything, afraid to live life on my own."

Connie nodded, her eyes soft.

"I just want some peace. My marriage and this Jessica have been totally consuming my thoughts. I'm sick of worrying, sick of not knowing."

"Huh," Connie said, chewing her wrap. She wore the face of someone who was thinking hard. "Jessica who? Do you know?"

"I don't know. Jessica Tate or something." Damn right it was; Dayna could picture the name written across the manila folder, a gold star next to it.

Connie tapped the table a few times with her long fingernail. "It's just, there's a Jessica Tate that works at Greg's office, answering phones, scheduling sessions, running coffee. You know, that sort of thing? I've met her a few times at different events. She's very pretty, but a little odd from what I hear." She shrugged. "It could be a different girl. I just—it's funny, funny as in strange, because Monica mentioned Greg recommended that this Jessica go see Richard, under Mark's advice of course. He wanted to treat her himself, but felt he was too close. Not objective enough."

Dayna's heart fluttered. "Why did Greg suggest she seek treatment?"

"I don't know much, just what I hear from Monica. But this Jessica seemed a bit unstable. Didn't have a strong work history. Always had different guys picking her up from the office. She came in crying a few mornings, once even with a black eye. Monica told Greg he should just fire her, you know how cruel she can be, it's the fashion model in her. But I think he felt bad. He suggested she talked to someone, said he knew just the guy."

A knot formed in Dayna's stomach. He'd known just the guy all right. "I guess that explains why she was at the party."

Connie nodded. "Greg probably invited her himself. A friendly gesture of sorts. I think she reminds him of his sister. You know? The one that killed herself. At least that's what Monica says."

"Unbelievable. Does she still work for Greg?"

"I think so."

Dayna stared at her untouched wrap but had lost her appetite.

"Keep your head up, honey. Don't let this thing eat away at you." Connie aimed a look at Dayna's plate then reached across the table and stole a fry.

"What would you do if Doug did this to you?" Dayna began. "You know, said he stopped the affair, then continued it anyway." Her mind returned to the other girls, but she still couldn't bring herself to mention them.

"I'd kill him," Connie said, laughing.

Chapter 17

After dinner with Connie, one glass of wine was not going to cut it. For a moment, she'd hated Greg, suspected he might be in on it too. The two of them passing women and pictures back and forth like sick fucks. But, deep down, she knew Greg was innocent. He hadn't intentionally sent Jessica to Richard knowing what he would do. He seemed to care for this girl, not want to hurt her. Plus, he had done it on a recommendation from Mark. As far as Dayna was concerned, Richard was solely responsible.

What she needed now was a drink, a distraction and a reminder that life keeps going even when you think it can't.

It was just after 8:30 p.m. on Wednesday night when she exited the cab in front of The Harborside. The dim lighting, the beautiful bar and the in your face, but somehow classy, nautical décor elicited a welcome wave of familiarity.

Dayna spotted him immediately. Sam sat on the right side of the bar, hunched, cradling a drink. His head was cocked up to see the wall-mounted TV. The Red Sox were playing some team she'd never heard of and didn't care about. Only two other men sat huddled at the bar watching the TV. One was sweating and kept rubbing his head; he probably had money on the game.

"I'm here every Wednesday and Friday," she pictured Sam saying as he smiled down at her. There had been no judgment in his smile, no prejudice against her age. He'd just seen her as another person to talk to, someone to pass the time with.

She settled next to him without saying a word and folded her arms in front of her. The granite bar top was cool and sticky against her forearms. Jimmy, the bartender from the other night, was on shift.

"Hey," she said.

Sam turned his head, nodded and returned his attention back to the game.

His face had shown no trace of surprise. Dayna fidgeted with her hands, her heart escalating. "Can I buy you a drink?" she asked.

"Sure," he said without meeting her gaze, then polished off the rest of his whiskey and slammed the glass down on the bar top.

Dayna wore a tight, black shirt that hugged her body and showed a playful hint of cleavage. More casual than her last appearance at The Harborside, she'd paired it with a simple skirt and heels. She wondered if Sam noticed her shirt, her hair, her perfume.

She waved at the bartender, pointed towards Sam, and held up two fingers. Jimmy prepared their drinks with the proficiency of an alchemist and slid two glasses towards them.

"Whiskey, huh?" Sam said, motioning to her glass.

She shrugged. "I figured I'd copy you this time."

He smiled, sipped his drink and stared back up at the television. Dayna nursed her own drink. The whiskey tasted of wood; she still hadn't acquired a liking for it.

"So, should we pretend it never happened?" Sam asked, his eyes never leaving the television.

What did he mean? The sex? Their meeting in the first place? She needed clarification. After all, she'd been messing up a lot lately. "That what never happened?"

He let out a grim chuckle. "Come on, Dayna, what's your angle? Did you come here to tell me you regret everything or that you drank too much and weren't thinking clearly?" He paused to sip his drink. "I get it, it's no big deal. But if you came here to beg me not tell anyone," he glanced down at her wedding ring, "you don't need to worry about that. Who would I even tell?"

"That's not why I'm here," she began, then paused. Why was she even here?

"Well, is it about my roommate? He said something about you pushing him."

Dayna winced. She suspected his roommate had probably used the words *crazy lady* or *old lady* to describe her. She didn't want Sam to think of her that way, even though she was probably both.

"I guess it doesn't matter. I just thought I'd never see you again and now here you are, buying me drinks. What am I supposed to make of this? Are you here to make up for assaulting my roommate or to see me?"

"I ..." She struggled to find the right thing to say. She hadn't expected him to be so forward.

"It's okay. We don't have talk about it. I get it. Life. Stress."

She glanced down at her wedding ring. After everything, she'd chosen to leave it on. She wasn't sure why. Maybe because she'd been married for so long? Maybe because she didn't want to answer questions from those who noticed? Maybe because she was still too afraid and lonely to leave?

Dayna brought her eyes to her whiskey and took a sip. The glass sweat left a liquid ring on the bar. A perfect circle. She traced it with her index finger.

Sam broke the silence first. "Do you want another drink?"

"No, I'm all set. I think I'll just head home."

"Did you take a cab here?"

She nodded.

"Come on. I'll give you a ride," he said, finishing his drink.

Sam was parked two blocks from the bar on a narrow side street. He seemed to have a talent for finding parking in a city with none. After nine on a Wednesday night, Boston was quiet and Dayna marveled how grey and still it appeared in the moonlight.

In the Toyota, Dayna glanced at the visor—the mirror was safely closed—then back down at her hands. "Twenty-six," she blurted.

About to turn the key, Sam dropped his hand into his lap. "Twenty-six what?" he asked.

For a second, she'd forgotten he was there, lost in her own head. "Twenty-six years. I've been married twenty-six fucking years."

Sam rotated towards her.

She wasn't sure if it was the genuine look of concern in his eyes or her general state of mind, but she swung her legs over the center console in a clumsy motion and straddled him.

Sam's breath exploded out of him. "What the hell?" he croaked.

She was surprised herself, but deep down, this must have been her intention all along, from the moment she decided to go back to the bar.

She started kissing him, but the hard, plastic steering wheel jamming into her back made things difficult. Sam leaned into her, squishing her further against the wheel, and a small grunt escaped her.

"Oops, just a sec," Sam said, reaching down. "Let me just get the..." The seat slipped back with a jerk. Their heads bumped generating laughter from them both. "Sorry about that."

"You can make it up to me," Dayna said.

He grinned and wrapped his arms around her. Their kissing resumed as his hands wandered to her breasts. Taking the cue, Dayna pulled off her shirt and he grabbed at them. Holding his face in her hands, she kissed his neck, then pushed herself against him, rocking back and forth.

He was erect, and she wanted him. With some maneuvering, she managed to unzip his pants, lift her skirt, and guide him into her. They both climaxed almost immediately. Sam groaned and shivered.

They stayed that way for a few moments trying to catch their breath. She grinned at him, then climbed back into the passenger's seat.

"You can take me home now," she said.

Chapter 18

Sam pulled up in front of her house a little after 10:00 p.m. Richard's bedroom light was still on and Dayna's breath caught in her throat.

"Nice place you got here," Sam said, with so much enthusiasm he had to be oblivious to her growing anxiety.

"Yeah," she muttered, reaching down to grab her purse and cell phone from the car floor. With her items gathered in her lap, they sat in silence, both waiting for the other to break it.

Sam spoke first. "Listen, I get this is… complicated, but I'll give you my number." His cheeks flushed. He took her cellphone from her lap and added himself as a contact, saving it under Sam, with no last name. Androgynous. "You know? In case you need a ride or anything." He grinned.

"Thanks," she said, smiling back.

She lifted herself out of the car and said another quick thank you before shutting the car door. She held the handle a moment, thinking, then yanked the door open just as the car began to move. The brakes squealed as it jerked to a stop.

"Sorry," she said. "Do you know what BPD means?"

He looked at her with a puzzled expression. "B. P. D." He enunciated each letter. "Blood pressure? No, that wouldn't explain the D." He repeated the letters a few more times. "Could D maybe stand for some type of disorder? Blood pressure disorder? Drop?"

Disorder. The word flashed in her head like a Las Vegas sign.

"Thanks," she said, shutting the door again.

He lowered the window. "What was that? A *Jeopardy* question?"

"Yeah," she said, giving him a wave before jogging up the driveway.

Inside, Dayna tossed her purse and shoes by the door. Her

hands were close to shaking, her mind moving at the speed of light. Her laptop sat in its usual place on the kitchen table. She opened it and pulled up Google. Stupid. Why hadn't she thought of doing this earlier? Maybe because part of her didn't really want to know what those three letters meant. Taking a deep breath, she typed BPD into the search engine.

Borderline Personality Disorder. She sat back and stared at the bright-blue letters. Borderline Personality Disorder.

She'd heard the phrase. Didn't Winona Ryder play a woman with borderline personality disorder in the movie *Girl Interrupted*? Dayna couldn't remember much about it, other than that the woman was in a nut house.

She scrolled down the page, searching for the most reliable link, preferably one that ended with *.org*. She chose one, scrolling to symptoms.

-Unstable personal relationships that alternate between devaluation and idealization.

-Unstable and distorted self-image, which can affect relationships, goals, opinions, values and moods.

-Impulsive behaviors, such as excessive spending, unsafe sex and/or substance abuse.

-Chronic feelings of boredom and emptiness.

-Suicidal and self-harming behavior.

-Frantic efforts to avoid abandonment by friends and family.

-Dissociative feelings.

Treatment options included psychotherapy and medication.

"Hmm," she grunted. Both were services Richard provided. She hit the back button and clicked into another link. This one focused on the higher levels of promiscuity found in borderlines.

Opening a new tab, she googled BPD and sex. Overwhelmed by the results, she clicked into one link, then another and another. Most articles hypothesized that some borderlines' high sex drives, promiscuity and impulsive sex acts were coping skills used to combat constant feelings of emptiness. One source said that feelings of boredom could also contribute to more sexual experimentation and casual sex. Articles went on to further mention higher incidents of borderlines being coerced into sex, being raped by strangers and catching STDs.

One article described themes found in a borderline's sexual behavior to include two words: *impulsivity* and *victimization*.

She stared at the words. Impulsivity and victimization. Being a psychiatrist, Richard was well versed in the diagnostic criteria of psychological disorders. He had to be in order to prescribe appropriate medication. He must have known he could take advantage of these girls' impulsivity, making them easy victims.

Jessica. Audrey. She'd been wrong about the girls. They weren't her enemies—they were victims. Her husband had listened to them talk and pretended to sympathize as he underlined key words cluing him into their diagnosis. Instead of helping them, Richard probably steered their conversations towards sex. He could have been gauging their perspectives— what they'd do and what they wouldn't. He manipulated them into trusting him. He knew they felt empty and chose to take advantage, using his dick to fill the void.

She slapped a hand on the desktop. When just fucking them wasn't enough, Richard had coerced them into taking naked pictures and saved them as souvenirs.

He was a monster.

Dayna startled when footsteps echoed above her, followed by creaking on the stairs. He was coming down. She slammed the laptop shut and sat rigid in the chair, her heart hammering.

Richard entered the kitchen. "Hello," he said, brushing past her to the fridge.

"Hello."

"You're home late." He poured himself a glass of water. "Should I be worried?"

"No. Of course not!"

"Good." He glanced at the closed laptop. "What are you

doing?"

"I thought about answering some emails, but I'm beat and it's pretty late."

His eyes narrowed; his bullshit detector was ticking into the danger zone. "It is pretty late," he echoed as he placed the water pitcher back in the fridge. "Well, goodnight, sweetheart."

She sat straighter, willing herself not to flinch as he bent to kiss her on the cheek before heading back upstairs.

Chapter 19

Dayna spent a good portion of the next morning pacing. At some point, she managed to shower and dress. Once that task was done, she returned to her pacing, wandering the halls and various rooms of the house while trying to keep the bile from rising into her throat.

Her thoughts were obsessive and replayed in a monotonous loop. While in the hall, her wedding picture caught her eye. She stopped and glared at the photo in the ornate frame. Richard stood, twenty years younger, a beaming smile on his face as he looked at her. She was returning the smile, their hands grasped in a loving embrace. They looked so happy. Yet, the longer she stared, the more the photo seemed to change. She had the impression she was looking at an entirely new picture, or at least a new version of the original. Now, a young, naive version of herself was gazing up at her new husband. Richard was still grinning, but his smile appeared forced. His eyes seemed darker than brown, almost like lumps of black coal, only smoother, like marbles. His gaze was cold and reptilian.

Dayna lifted the picture from its nail and heaved it down the hall. The pretty frame snapped and glass shattered on the hardwood floor. The picture slid from its glass cell and came to rest on the floor where it belonged.

Dayna's grandmother only took baths. For much of her childhood, Dayna thought it was something all old people did, but she learned otherwise when eighty-year-old Mrs. Bradbury down the street mentioned how much she used her shower. When Dayna asked her grandmother about it, she said baths were more soothing than showers. Baths allowed her to relax. She claimed soaking in still water calmed the skin and the mind. Water flooding out of a faucet onto her head was too harsh and too violent for her. She said it reminded her of being trapped in a thunderstorm and she couldn't understand why folks, as she called them, ran from the rain but willingly stood in a shower.

Dayna thought of her grandmother now as she luxuriated in the hot water streaming over her head, shoulders, and down her back. Clouds of steam filled the enclosure, and droplets raced down the walls. She welcomed the illusion of being immersed in a tropical rainstorm, with water so hot it almost burned her skin and turned her flesh a rosy pink.

Dayna had left the bathroom door open in case Richard came home early, hoping she'd hear his footfalls or the clink of his keys on the table in the foyer. Closing her eyes, she raised her face towards the shower head and let the water beat down on her. All she wanted was to relax and not think about anything for just a few moments. Perhaps this was what drug addicts desired right before they slid the needle into their flesh, muting their feelings and rendering their thoughts momentarily silent.

And it worked.

For a few minutes, the water was just loud enough to drown out her thoughts and just hot enough to distract her from her obsessing. But like a drug, the effect was only temporary and thoughts of Richard's deceit crept back into her mind.

Her eyes fluttered open, trying to adjust to the glaring white of the tile and expanding steam around her. As she shifted to let the water hit the back of her neck, a patch of black passed on the other side of the sheer shower curtain.

The lights flickered. Dayna jumped back against the tile. The surface seemed frigid against her upper shoulders and back, but she couldn't move. That momentary shadow had not been Richard. She strained to hear over the now overwhelming sound of water.

The lights flickered again—then remained off. Heart pounding, Dayna stood in total darkness. The figure was here. Not in a mirror. Not in a window. She could sense its powerful presence.

She waited in terrified anticipation for cold, dead fingers to reach through the curtains. In some ways, she wanted them to come. To get it over with was better than waiting.

Standing in silence, she wondered if this was how she would die, trapped in a shower, slowly scorching to death under scalding hot water. She strained to see through the darkness, but her attempts were useless. She needed to move if there was any hope of escaping the figure. She reached for the curtain with her left hand. When her fingers brushed the fabric, she recoiled as if stung, jolted by an unexpected pain.

She screamed as the lights snapped on, blinding her for an instant. When her sight returned, a dark entity stood on the other side of the curtain.

There was a small, warm drip on her foot. Not warm like water or urine, but thick and heavy. Looking down, she saw blood. A perfect crimson petal rested on her big toe and rose-colored water pooled around her feet. Her right hand held her razor. Her left arm was torn and scraped at the wrist.

She cried out and the razor clattered to the shower floor. Surely she hadn't done that to herself. In desperation, she flung her wrist under the shower, gasping at the sting from the hot water. The wound was not deep, but enough to draw blood. A small section of skin was pulled back, the soft flesh beneath it exposed. She whirled to face the intruder, but the figure had vanished. Was this what happened when insanity loomed?

She took a deep breath, turned off the water, and peeked out. The bathroom was empty. On the tile floor, a path of wet footprints began at the shower's edge, leading to the sink where the medicine chest hung open. A box of extra razors lay on its side. Dayna stared at the footprints. They couldn't possibly belong to her. She would have remembered if she had left the shower, wouldn't she?

She looked down at the blood trickling off her foot. She

clamped a hand over her wrist and stepped out, trying to avoid dropping blood onto the white towel she'd left ready for use.

A trail of pinpoint crimson droplets marked the pathway from the shower to the toilet where she yanked the role of toilet paper from its holder and struggled to wind it around her wound. She wondered whether she needed stiches or if her makeshift bandage would hold up.

She pulled a black, long-sleeved shirt over her head in attempt to conceal her mutilated wrist. Her heart was still clapping in her chest. She couldn't live like this anymore. The game had been taken to a new level, her bloody wound proved that. The idea of this *thing* being a ghost was more than just a flirtation, it was evolving into a fact. There seemed to be no pattern to its appearances and no clues as to why. But of one fact she was certain: the dark figure wasn't a problem until the day she had set foot into that motel.

She slipped into some black pants and grabbed a pair of heels from the closet. Down the hall, she skirted the shattered remains of her wedding photo. She snatched her purse and keys, hurried to the car, and backed out of the driveway. She kept her eyes lowered, in case the figure was watching out the upstairs window.

Chapter 20

Zig-zagging through Newton, Dayna shot onto Route 9, following the road to I-95 south. Familiarity washed over her as she made her way down the long strip of highway. Despite the stinging in her wrist, the grey of the asphalt and green of the trees put her in an almost hypnotic trance. Forty minutes later, she pulled off the same exit she took that Saturday a month ago.

The streets became more rural, lined with small Capes and Colonials. The seventy-degree weather had the neighborhood kids outside. Girls drew hopscotch squares on driveways and boys ran wild through sprinklers. A few teenagers took turns throwing a ball through a basketball hoop. They paused their game as she passed, looking at her with inquisitive eyes. Dayna imagined them filling in the empty street after she drove by, yelling "car" whenever the danger presented itself, interfering with their game.

At the next intersection, she took a left and followed a blue sign promising gas, Dunkin Donuts, McDonald's and lodging. A few miles later she spotted the motel, its flashing vacancy sign just visible beyond McDonald's golden arches.

Her tires screeched as she made a sharp and deliberate left into the spot nearest the motel's office. Throwing her car into park, she peered up at the sign. THE GREEN GARDEN MOTEL loomed over her in neon brilliance.

The office stank of cigarettes and moth balls, a nauseating combination. The room was bare aside from a rack of pamphlets depicting Massachusetts's local attractions, some of which were more than two hours away. The front desk was empty, forcing Dayna to ring the bell labeled 'RING ONCE FOR SERVICE'. She rang it three times.

She was staring at a yellowing, off-centered picture of a flower when the door behind the desk creaked open. She half expected to see Norman Bates step out calling for "Mother." To her dismay, it was the same man from that Saturday before, greasy Mick, still donning his nametag which read 'MICK, HAPPY TO HELP'. She hated him.

"Can I help you, ma'am?" he asked with no indication that he was, in fact, happy to help.

"I need to take a look in room forty-two."

"How many nights?" he asked, meandering his way to the computer.

"No, no. I just need to look in it. I—I left my wedding ring here a few weeks ago."

"Yup, that happens a lot here. But anything we find, rings and such, we put in our lost and found." He turned from her and reached under the desk revealing a cardboard box with the words 'LOST AND FOUND' written in sloppy handwriting across the front. "What'd you say it looked like again?"

"No, I—it's not in there. I just need to see the room." She was pleading with him.

He studied her, his lips turning down at the corners.

"Please," Dayna said again. She tried using her blue eyes to her advantage, flashing him an innocent look, but they felt hot from where tears threatened to fall.

Mick brought his attention back to the computer, clicked the mouse a few times, saying nothing. He looked from the computer to her, then back at the screen. "All right, you have five minutes. I have people checking in at 7:00."

Dayna's eyes found the wall-mounted clock above his head which read 6:50. "Thanks. I really appreciate it."

"Come on. I'll walk you over there."

Dayna followed Mick with growing anxiety. His slow waddle kept them at a frustrating pace and she was thankful the room was located on the first floor.

When they approached room 42, greasy Mick displayed a white key card and with a single swipe of plastic she was back in the motel room, greeted by the same flowered bedspread, plaid curtains and faint odor of cigarettes.

"All right, five minutes. I mean it."

For a moment, Dayna thought he was going to stand there and supervise her, documenting her every move. But he simply turned around and muttered something about manning the phones because somebody had to do it.

As soon as he was out of sight, Dayna headed for the bathroom. The fluorescent lights hit her with their familiar buzz. She rested both hands on the counter and leaned forward, her face only a few inches from the glass.

"Come on, you bastard," Dayna said. The hot air from her mouth left a thin fog on the mirror where she'd first glimpsed the dark figure. She was staring so hard her eyes began to water. "Come on," she whispered again.

She held that position for what felt like a solid two minutes before concluding nothing was going to happen. She had been sure this would work. Well, maybe not sure, but hopeful.

She sighed out of frustration. The bright white of the bathroom was becoming menacing, causing a thin sweat to break out on her forehead. She leaned back, allowing her posture to relax when the figure darted behind her, disappearing into the dark bedroom. Dayna hinged forward and craned her neck to the left, hoping to gain a better vantage point into the mirror. Without luck, she tore her gaze from the glass. The room felt ten degrees cooler.

She stepped into the bedroom and the bathroom door slammed shut behind her, rattling a picture. Dayna whirled around; the sweat on her forehead turned cold and clammy. *Get a hold of yourself*, Dayna. The temperature drop, the slamming door, this figure, all had to be some type of sick trick. And if they weren't, there had to be something more, some reason this *thing* had attached itself to her.

She felt an icy wind as the entity swooshed behind her and into the closet. Dayna yanked open the closet door finding nothing but a small ironing board and three metal hangers secured to the rod. The figure passed behind her again. She wheeled around to see it vanish by the dresser. She ran over and pulled out every drawer with such force the lamp balanced on top came crashing down. But before she could react, the figure circled to her right and dissolved into the armchair. Dayna removed the cushion and examined its underside, hoping to find a demonic symbol, a pentagram, anything. But there was nothing. She threw the cushion aside and turned to find the figure seated on the bed.

"Stop following me," Dayna said boldly, but she felt her initial determination and courage slipping. She walked backwards until her butt bumped the dresser the TV sat on. "Stay away." Reaching behind her, she found the remote and threw it at the figure. It passed through the figure's torso and slammed against the wall, batteries flying. The black figure melted into the bed, much as it had that day in the stream.

"No," she cried as she ran to the bed, tearing at the sheets, throwing pillows. "No. No." After driving all this way, she was not going to lose this thing again, not until she knew it was gone for good. Dayna peered under the bed, finding nothing but dust.

"Look at this place!"

She popped her head up. Greasy Mick was standing in the open doorway.

"I remember you now. You were here about a month ago, completely trashed this room and cost us over two hundred dollars in damages." He exhaled through his nose in disbelief and disgust. "What exactly do you think you're doing?"

The question enraged her and she practically jumped to her feet. "What am I doing? What the hell do you think you're doing? Is this some kind of sick joke you play on your customers? Is it?" she screamed, her finger pointing at him in accusation as her heart hammered in her chest.

"I don't know what you're talking about, lady."

"No, of course not. No one ever knows what I am talking about. It's all in my head. But I know what I saw. I saw it just now, in this room, right here." She pointed at the bed.

"What did you see, exactly? A dinosaur?"

She opened her mouth and closed it. What had she seen? A ghost? "I think... I think I saw a ghost."

Mick looked around the room. "Well, all I see is a mess," he said, finally. His expression hardening. "Listen, lady, I don't know what kind of stuff you're on, but you need to get the fuck outta here before I call the police. I mean it."

Dayna wanted to cry but couldn't. She was too shocked by his total disbelief and lack of concern. She didn't really know what it was she expected. Maybe for him to tell her to sit down and offer her a glass of water? Maybe for him to humor her and take a look around? Maybe for him to tell her he knew a guy, who knew a guy, who dabbled in this sort of thing? Isn't that what was supposed to happen?

"You're a real asshole," she yelled before pushing past him, almost colliding with a man and woman holding suitcases.

"What about the damages? It's at least another hundred," Mick called after her.

"Bill me," she screamed and ran to her car, ignoring the incredulous looks from the few onlookers in the parking lot.

Trembling hands made it almost impossible to get the key into the ignition and start the car. She was more furious and confused than ever. At the hum of the engine, she threw her car into reverse and tore out of the gravel parking lot leaving an uprising of dirt and dust behind her.

She caught one last glimpse of greasy Mick, standing where she'd left him, the door to room 42 still open. His hands were waving over his head, his face red, mouth open.

Reversing her route, Dayna took a right at the intersection, following green signs for I-95 North to Boston. Dark was approaching quickly as she raced towards the teenagers gathered in front of the basketball hoop. One made a throw, missed, and the ball bounced off the backboard, rolling into the street. Dayna slammed on her brakes. One of the boys jogged to pick up the ball, throwing her a wave. She sat, breathing hard, her hands welded to the steering wheel. She managed to nod at the kid before he tossed the ball back to his buddies and jogged away. That was too close; she needed to relax. She continued down the street at a reasonable pace. The sun vanishing as she took the on-ramp for I-95 North.

Chapter 21

Less than thirty minutes into her drive, twilight became full dark and the moon, hidden by clouds, cast only a thin light through the night sky. With no streetlights, Dayna had to rely solely on her headlights, which glistened off the white dotted line. As she stared at the center line, she understood why truckers worried about white line fever; she forced herself to look ahead into the darkness—into nothing.

Her left arm throbbed. Probably, the wound had started to bleed again. Ignoring it, she reached across to the passenger's seat for her purse, managing to remove her Marlboro's and lighter. She slipped a cigarette from the pack and lit it. On the radio, Elton John's *Benny and the Jets* turned into *Dreams* by Fleetwood Mac and Dayna turned up the volume. Cracking a window, she exhaled smoke into the cool night air.

Dayna snuck a quick glance in the rearview mirror. A falling tear formed a wet trail down the side of her left cheek. The area under her eyes was blackened from mascara. Shit, she looked a little like a fucking mime. Holding her cigarette and the wheel in one hand, she wiped under her eyes, trying to erase any evidence of her tears. She checked the rearview again, satisfied.

What a waste! Her mission had brought no answers, no clues. Now, she could only pray the figure would stay at the motel. A silly thought, but maybe the figure was like a lost dog: once it was brought back home, it would stay put. If it didn't, she had serious problems.

For instance, maybe the figure was only a figment of her imagination, some darkness she carried around inside her own head. Richard, the big shot psychiatrist, would have a field day with that. She didn't think that was the case, but you never knew.

Up ahead, a young woman standing on the side of the highway came into Dayna's line of sight. Visibility was tough in the dark, but her headlights illuminated the woman's small frame, maybe twenty feet in front of her. Her skin was shockingly pale against her long, black hair. Her arms were crossed around her abdomen, hugging her skimpy tank top.

Dayna's heart quickened. Pedestrians were not allowed on highways. She edged her foot off the brake, slowing the car, fearing the young woman would run into the road, but she made no movement. Dayna searched the rearview mirror, but the girl had remained where she was.

Dayna's heart thudded. Perhaps the woman's car had broken down. But where was the car? Could the woman be walking in search of help? With no exit for at least three miles, Dayna slowed to fifty, she should help the poor girl. But what if it was a set up? Some thieving thugs could be using a young, pretty girl as bait, waiting for some innocent idiot to stop and lend a hand. Dayna did not want to be that idiot. Her hands shook and the cigarette slipped from between her fingers and rolled beneath her feet.

"Fuck. Fuck. Fuck." Her eyes bounced from the road down to the floor. The cigarette rested by her left foot, she could just make it out in the dim light emanating from the dashboard. Dayna eased off the gas, letting the car slow. Her left hand strained to reach the cigarette. She felt the heat radiating from one end and carefully pinched it in the middle. Quickly, she tossed the cigarette through the cracked window, sighing in relief.

Her gaze returned to the road. What the hell? Another young woman—the other's twin—was in the center of the highway, dead ahead. Dayna cranked the wheel right. The car vibrated as the tires crossed the rumble strip. A wall of pine trees appeared in front of her. Slamming on the brakes, she turned the wheel, hard and fast. The seatbelt tightened around her. One of her tires exploded, causing the car to swerve before coming to a sudden, shaking stop.

She leaned back in the seat. Hands in a death grip on the

steering wheel, she sat still, breathing hard. Her heart was slamming against her ribs like it wanted to escape. After a moment, she eased her foot off the brake. She wasn't dead: that was good. *Dreams* still floated through the quiet car. She shifted the gear into park and turned off the ignition silencing the song. The woman.

Dayna peered into the driver's side mirror, then the passenger's where she spotted her a few feet behind the car, her arms still wrapped around her stomach. She was kneeling on the pavement, with her head slumped forward.

Dayna jumped from the car, looked at the woman, then past her down the road. Two identical women didn't make sense. But how could the woman have gotten in front of her?

"Are you okay?" she yelled. "Are you hurt?"

The closer Dayna got, unreality crept in. The woman lifted her head and Dayna froze. The woman's face held no expression, but her eyes... her eyes terrified her. There was nothing behind them. No light, no emotion. They were like the eyes of a doll.

The girl's face began to change, her features melting, her pale skin darkening and wrinkling. Her long black hair transformed into a hood's velvety fabric. The girl rose, metamorphosing into the black figure. For an instant, it stood facing Dayna, then lifted a hand and pulled down its hood. For the first time, Dayna gazed at the figure's exposed head. It was the face of an old woman: dark, horrifying, with eyes a sickly grey, pupils solid black.

Dayna took a step back. The woman laughed, a hideous cackle that pierced the silence.

Dayna gasped, putting a hand over her mouth. The woman vanished, the sound of her cackle lingering in the air before fading away.

Dayna stared, then turned and sprinted to the car. The Chevy sat on the gravel shoulder. The back tire on the driver's side was flat. She glanced back to where the woman had been. What the hell was that? A figment of her imagination? The devil?

She shivered and turned back to the Chevy. She knew how to jack a car up to change a tire but getting to the spare and tools would be tricky. There wasn't much room on the loose gravel for the jack's base. She looked down the road, seeing no other cars, no streetlights, nor the distant friendly glow of a house through the trees. She couldn't imagine walking. It would be too dangerous in the dark, and almost impossible in her heels.

She got back into the car and locked the doors. Not that it would do much good. If that thing really was the devil, mechanical door locks would not stop it.

She couldn't help glancing in the mirror, and almost melted with relief at seeing the back seat empty. She found her purse on the passenger seat and hunted through it for her cell phone. She pulled it free and tapped it on. The familiar glow of the screen welcomed her and she felt an inkling of normality returning.

Her finger hovered over Max's name. Staring at her peach fingernail, she tried to steady her hands. Dayna did not want her son to see her like this. What would she even say? There would be too many questions, too many concerned looks. He would want to call Richard. Sighing, she scrolled down, found Sam's name, and dialed it.

He answered, on the fourth ring. "Hello?"

"I need you to come pick me up." Her voice quivered, close to tears.

"Dayna? Where are you? What's going on?"

"I don't know. I'm somewhere off 95, on the northbound side. Maybe twenty minutes south of the city."

"What—"

"An accident," she said.

"I'm on my way."

"Please hurry."

Chapter 22

Her cellphone's clock read 9:25 p.m. Where was Sam? Each car that passed sent her heart into an unsteady rhythm. She was eager with anxious anticipation. Her lower back ached from sitting rigid in the car's uncomfortable leather seat for almost thirty minutes. She'd resisted turning on the radio, not sure how long car batteries lasted; same with the interior lights. She longed to banish the darkness surrounding her but felt uncomfortable with the thought that any passing driver seeing a lone woman in a car could be a threat. What was worse, having an evil spirit in the car with her or being raped and killed by brutes out for a joyride?

Headlights streamed into her car's windows. Someone was pulling up on the shoulder beside her. She shielded her eyes as the car stopped. With great relief, she saw Sam step out of his Toyota.

Dayna scrambled out and met him halfway. She threw her arms around him in a strong embrace, tears spewing from her eyes.

"Thank you for coming," she said, taking a step back and releasing him from her desperate hug.

"Jesus, Dayna. You're bleeding. Are you okay?" Sam reached for her wrist, but she pulled it back. A small trail of blood, appearing black in the glare of the headlights, must have leaked through the toilet paper bandage on the back of her hand.

"It's nothing. I'm fine." She yanked her sleeve down and hid the injured hand behind her back.

"What's going on? Did you hit something?"

"I went off the side of the road. My tire blew and—well, I didn't know who else to call. I'm sorry." Hysteria threatened.

"Are you okay? Hurt?"

"I'm fine… sort of. I thought I saw a woman in the road. She came out of nowhere. I swerved to avoid her and lost control."

"There was a woman on the highway? Did you hit her? Is *she* okay?" Sam asked, alarm creeping into his voice, each question sounding more urgent than the last.

"No. I didn't hit her. She—well—I don't even think," Dayna paused. "I don't even think she was really there. I know how it sounds, I just—"

"Dayna, have you been drinking? Did you take anything?"

"No, I didn't take anything. I'm tired, that's all." The tears began to fall again. "I'm just shaken up."

He reached out and pulled her into him. "It's okay. We will figure this out, okay?"

She nodded not wanting to move her head from his chest, feeling safe for the first time in weeks despite the traces of uncertainty she detected in his voice.

He led her back to her car, then steadied her before walking around it to survey the damage.

"Well, I could change the tire, but the tire on the other side looks low. Probably leaking from grit between the tire and the rim. Often happens if you go into a sideways skid. I'll give you a ride home. You can call a tow truck in the morning."

It was a quiet ride back with only the soft hum of the radio filling the silence. Dayna leaned a heavy head against the cool glass window to keep it from toppling from her body and falling onto the car floor.

"Do you want to stay at my place?" Sam asked.

She marshaled the energy to lift her head. They were already back in Newton, approaching her street.

"I can't. I want to, but I've been out almost every night this week. I don't want my husband to get suspicious. I can't deal with his questions, not tonight." It wasn't exactly the truth, but she feared admitting she was deathly tired. Not to mention she suspected she was slowly bleeding to death from cuts she'd bandaged with toilet paper instead of getting stiches.

"Since when do you care about what your husband thinks?" he asked as he took the sharp left down her road.

She glared at him. "Don't do that."

"Sorry," he said.

But Dayna detected the edge of frustration in his voice.

When they pulled up in front of her house the kitchen light was on. She might have forgotten to turn it off—anything was possible—but she had a strong feeling it was Richard waiting up for her.

She took a moment to gather her remaining strength. She rubbed a couple of fingers under each eye once more in an attempt to erase any melted makeup—not that she dared to pull down the visor to check. She ran her fingers through her hair and fluffed her loose curls, trying to assume the outward image of somebody normal, somebody who wasn't being driven insane by some sort of *ghost*. She hated to use the word, but signs seemed to be pointing her to that conclusion.

Sam rested a gentle hand on her thigh. "Promise me you'll be okay?"

"I can't make any promises," she said, throwing him a soft smile. "But I'll sure as hell try." She reached for the door handle. "Thanks again for getting me. I feel so stupid."

"You know you can talk to me, right? I'm here for you. You don't have to keep it to yourself and be so damn mysterious all the time." He paused. "I've been thinking about what you said back on the highway. I want you to know that I believe you about the woman, that you really saw her. Probably just some crazy, strung out bitch, who took off after you crashed."

"Probably." Dayna smiled and patted his hand. She leaned towards him and gave him a long kiss. He believed her. He had helped her, climbing out of bed to drive out and pick her up on the side of the road. One day soon she'd figure out some other way to repay him, but for now a simple kiss would have to suffice. "Goodnight," she said softly.

"Goodnight, Dayna."

She didn't look back as she heard Sam pull away. Didn't wave. She was too distracted by the flicker of the side door's blinds. Richard was watching.

Chapter 23

She did not acknowledge Richard when she entered the house, taking the time to hang her purse on the coat rack and slip off her heels in the entryway.

Her husband sat at the kitchen table with a few books spread out before him and an almost empty glass of whiskey. In that moment, Dayna wished for the power of invisibility, unsure if she could handle this confrontation.

Richard shot up at the sight of her, unsteady on his feet. He removed his reading glasses and set them on the table. Dayna held back laughter, remembering she used to find him sexy in his glasses.

"Are you having an affair?" he asked, breaking the silence with slurred words.

"What? Are you waiting up for me now?" She winced, probably sounding like a sneaky teenager lying to their parents.

"That's not an answer, Dayna."

She sighed. "I went out with the girls. Monica dropped me off."

"I'm a few things, sweetheart, but I'm not dumb. Monica wouldn't be caught dead in a Toyota. Now... I'm asking you again. Are you having an affair?" He took a swig of his drink. "And how about a little honesty."

Her heart fluttered, her legs weak. Richard had watched her from the window, seen her kiss Sam. Now he was testing her, seeing how long she would keep up this charade. She should have stayed the night at Sam's.

Skirting him at a safe distance, she moved to the counter. She faced him, using the support of the counter to compensate for her weak legs. She eyed the half-empty bottle of Crown Royale next to the fridge. "And what if I am?" She tried to sound confident, but her voice shook.

"I knew it." He laughed. "I fucking knew it."

He began to pace, a nervous habit. He stopped. "You can see how this is hypocritical? You can see that right?" His voice was edging closer to a yell. He resumed the pacing.

She snorted. It was a common theme, replayed and acted out in movies, TV shows, and books. Husband cheats on wife, she's forced to deal with it. Wife cheats on husband and he loses his fucking mind.

Dayna jumped as an angry buzz and cadence of electronic chimes burst from Richard's cell phone on the kitchen table. Richard cast an angry glance towards it. He took a step to the left, shielding it with his body as if to block the sound, but the phone continued to ring and vibrate against the wooden table.

"I'm trying here. I'm trying so damn hard," he said and swallowed more whiskey. The interruption of the cellphone appeared to have softened him. He took a step forward and the phone's whining ceased, giving off one last electronic beep as it indicated a new voicemail.

"I see you're sticking with that story," Dayna said. "Can you look me in the eyes and sincerely tell me you're not seeing Jessica? That there were no other girls, sick girls who you manipulated?" It was her turn to be angry. Richard had no right to be furious with her after everything he'd done.

He let out a laugh. "I didn't make those girls do anything they didn't want to. They were practically begging for it."

The whiskey had clearly taken control, allowing his secrets to slip. His coldness staggered her, even though it'd been there all along, probably since the beginning of their marriage.

"You're a fucking monster. You deserve to lose your license." Her voice was calm, but Richard looked as if she had slapped him across the face, his eyes bulging in shock.

"Are you fucking..." He paused, raising a hand to his forehead which had broken into a thin sweat. He squeezed his eyes shut. With a deep inhalation, his eyes fluttered open and his hand dropped back to his side. "Honey, you still seem to be confused," he began. "You haven't been well. I've stuck by your side and this is the thanks I get. I should have just left you and saved myself the misery. You're the problem here, not me."

"Are you serious?"

"You'll be sorry." He polished off the rest of his drink. "You'll be so fucking sorry."

Dayna glared at him. No way was he going to back pedal out of this. He was attempting to manipulate her again, but this time she knew it. Now she wondered just how much of his own lies he actually believed.

"Screw you," she said and raised her hand to slap him. But he was quick, catching her wrist midair. She tore it free from his grasp. For an instant, she held her breath. She could imagine him taking her by the throat, slamming her head into the counter, cracking the bottle over her skull, but he didn't do anything. He barely moved.

After a moment, he grabbed his cellphone from the table, advanced towards her, and stood two inches from her face. She could smell the whiskey strong and sour on his breath. She braced herself for the violence, willing herself to stand her ground.

"Whore," he said, grabbing the bottle of Crown Royale from behind her with so much force it made her flinch, and marched out.

Dayna stood motionless, listening to the side door slam and the Porsche start up and whip out of the driveway down their quiet Newton street. She leaned back against the counter, exhausted.

Eventually, she managed to drag herself up the stairs to her bedroom. She pulled off her dress and rummaged through the dresser drawer for pajamas, craving their soft fabric and warmth against her skin.

Some time later—she didn't know how long—she found

herself in bed, the sheets half on, half off. She couldn't remember getting into bed. Her body was covered in a thick sweat. Her underwear was off and there was wetness between her legs. She wondered if it was sweat or urine but was too tired to care. She settled back into a dark, unsettling sleep consumed by nightmares.

In her dream, there was water. Where she was, she wasn't quite sure. She just knew she was somewhere wet, somewhere that didn't feel safe. A man's yell came faint in the distance, then an unfamiliar scent. 'Burnt' was the only word that came to mind.

Dayna jerked awake, her heart thundering in her chest. The thought of a heart attack crossed her mind then dissipated. She listened for sounds of Richard, but the house was silent. Yet, for just a moment, she was sure she still smelled the strange, burnt scent from her dream.

Chapter 24

Cooking for one was much easier than cooking for two. The adjustment had been strange at first, but just as she'd learned to cook for two instead of three after Max first fled the nest, she got the hang of it. In fact, she rather enjoyed it. No more worrying about not adding mushrooms or green peppers. Red, yellow, and orange were fine, but Richard detested green.

Dinner was in front of the TV with the fireplace lit. Pouring herself a generous glass of white wine, she watched *Jeopardy* while she ate.

It had been four days since she had last spoken to her husband. Four days since she decided she would no longer be making dinner, or any other meal for that matter, for Richard. Four days since she'd spoken to Connie's lawyer friend, Ron Scheinberg, who told her he would love to sit down with her sometime next week and chat. But more importantly, it had been four days since she'd last seen the figure.

Apparently, their last confrontation had been enough for Richard, too. He'd even adjusted his schedule, staying at work later, giving her enough time to watch Alex Trebek ask contestants questions he, himself, would never know the answers to at 7:30 p.m.

After dinner, Dayna had been going to Sam's where she either spent the night or came home late enough that she could sneak upstairs to her room undetected in the dark. Tonight, would be no different. Sam didn't mind. He'd told her two nights ago, after a few drinks, that his nights with her were what he looked forward to all day.

For a Monday, finding parking by Sam's apartment was more difficult then she'd anticipated and Dayna regretted not taking a cab. Early May meant the spring semester was ending, giving college kids yet another excuse to party, even if it was the beginning of the week.

Sam's neighborhood was packed to capacity with cars. He lived by a few of the city's more popular bars and, apparently, people would rather drink and drive then take the extra five minutes to wait for a cab or bus.

People were scattered everywhere and the neighborhood was filled with noise: cars honking, distant music, people laughing. A homeless man was beating a drum set of overturned buckets, with a hat out in front for any aficionado of random rhythms.

The Boston area was already famous for pedestrians jaywalking in front of green lights during broad daylight, but the scene was close to madness in an area with hordes of drunk college kids walking around at night. When a girl in heels like stilts stumbled into the street about ten feet ahead of her car, Dayna stomped on the brakes and screeched to a stop.

"Ya fuckin' idiot," someone yelled from the sidewalk.

"You got that right," Dayna mumbled, hands glued to the wheel. Although whether the shouter was referring to the girl or to her, Dayna wasn't sure. She gritted her teeth, waiting for the stupid young woman to totter out of her lane before continuing.

After circling around the block three more times, she found an open spot. She locked the car and strolled the half-block to Sam's building, feeling as though all eyes were on her. She had to be a generation older than everyone else around.

Right next to Boston University, Allston was a college town. Trash littered the streets, blown in from overflowing dumpsters and trashcans. She skirted cigarette butts, gum blobs and junk food wrappers as she walked.

She stepped off the walk outside Sam's building and rang his buzzer. Three young girls with their arms linked brushed past her indifferently, their long legs exposed by short, black dresses. They left behind a scent of perfume, bubble gum and vodka. She felt a pang of envy as they sauntered away, laughing. So naïve;

not a care in the world.

She jumped at the loud buzz of the front door, yanked open the door and started up the stairs. By the third floor, Dayna was out of breath. How she and Sam had ever managed to make this climb drunk on that first night together was still a mystery to her. Two floors to go.

"Do you need me to call the paramedics?" came Sam's voice down the stairwell.

"Very funny," she called back. "When are you moving to a place with an elevator?"

Sam greeted her at the door with a hug, an action she always had a hard time returning without embarrassment. She couldn't help glancing past him, worried about meeting his roommate. So far, Sam had made sure that the kid she'd pushed to the floor had been nowhere in sight when Dayna arrived. She dreaded another encounter with someone who saw her as old enough to be Sam's mother. Still, she felt the familiar thrill, that little spark of adventure when she was with Sam. Or was it payback to Richard?

She placed her purse on Sam's cheap IKEA desk. Every time she was in his room, she spotted something new. Yesterday, it was a beer stein with beautifully intricate designs. Sam told her his dad had brought it back for him from Germany, straight from the source and therefore too nice to use. Today, her eyes fell to the poster above Sam's desk: a striking young woman in a thin nightgown so loose it fell off her shoulders, one breast exposed. The girl's eyes were directed outward, as if challenging Dayna to explain what Sam was doing with someone Dayna's age when he could have her.

"So, I was thinking we could do something different tonight," Sam said. "Maybe go out for a stroll? We could go down by the river."

She smiled. He sounded like a nervous boy asking a girl out for a first date.

The last four nights they'd sat in bed, consumed a few drinks, and had sex. After, they spent some time talking until they fell asleep or Dayna left. At least he wasn't sick of her—yet.

Dayna couldn't help glancing at the picture again. "I don't think that's a good idea. I mean, someone could see us and… you and me…" She felt herself aging by the second. "This might be hard to explain."

Mentally, she crossed her fingers. Would he be as embarrassed as her if they ran across an acquaintance of his?

"I guess you're right," he said. "We should stay here and watch a movie. We could order a pizza later, if we're hungry." He flashed his big boyish grin.

Thirty minutes later, they were snuggled in Sam's bed eating Peter's Pizza Palace, watching *Fight Club*. Sam had bubbled over it so much while looking though his DVDs that Dayna had hidden her reluctance. When she admitted she hadn't seen it, Sam assured her that she'd love it. "First rule of fight club is: you do not talk about fight club," he said, apparently quoting some character. "The second rule of fight club is: you do not talk about fight club."

Sam had dragged the bureau holding his 42inch TV and gaming system to the foot of the bed, claiming it would give them a more comfortable viewing experience with a cinema-like feel. He poured them each a glass of Jack Daniels. Despite her distaste for whiskey, she was certainly drinking a lot of it these days.

"I can't believe you've never seen this movie," Sam said.

She shrugged. "Guess I never got around to it."

"Well, I expected better of you. It came out in 1999. You're way behind the times, lady."

He laughed, but Dayna didn't. Sam had been nine years old when the movie premiered and she thirty-one.

"Hey, don't get all bent out of shape about it. It's not that big of a deal that you're a loser."

She dropped her mouth in pretended shock and punched his chest. Sam had a nonchalant attitude making her forget things were ever a big deal. It was an innocence she craved and admired. He was forcing her to watch *Fight Club* because it was a cult classic he truly thought she needed to see to better her quality of life.

They didn't make it to the end of the movie before passing on the pizza and going straight to the sex. She was surprised by how easily she surrendered to Sam's touch, like a horny teenager with hormones raging. In the beginning, she used to think of Richard, sometimes even see his face, his dark eyes glaring at her from where Sam's should have been. But each session with Sam made it easier to push Richard from her mind.

Chapter 25

Morning light filtered into Sam's room, sneaking through gaps in the curtains. The abrasive, enthusiastic sounds of night had taken on a more subdued tone. The homeless man's drumming had been replaced by quiet talking and the light sound of alternative rock drifting from cafes and bars now open for breakfast, although the smell of alcohol still hung heavy in the air.

Sam lay in bed next to her, not yet wakened by his alarm set for work. Dayna wished he didn't have to go, but it was a Tuesday.

Tuesday. The word sent a surge of panic through Dayna's body. She shot up so fast the bed shook, waking Sam.

"Christ, what's wrong?" he asked, rolling on his side to face her. "Do you have crime to fight somewhere, Batman?"

"Fuck," she said, already up, reaching for her shirt and pulling on pants.

Sam sighed. "Would you like to share with the class what's going on?"

"It's Tuesday," she said, as if it explained everything.

"Yeah, it is," he said, glancing at the alarm clock. "Five minutes before my alarm, in fact."

She glared at him. "I have this dinner tonight with my husband and his friend, well more like his mentor—it doesn't matter. It's been planned for weeks. I don't even want to go. I just—"

"Don't go then," Sam said. He sighed and brought a pillow over his head, shielding his eyes from the expanding morning light.

"It's not that easy. I have to go." She did not want to elaborate. Nor did she want to explain her plan to divorce Richard. Sam might get a big head and think she was doing it for him, which she certainly was not. What Sam didn't understand was, if she did not show up to this dinner with Mark and Marilyn, Richard would be suspicious. As far as he knew this "fight" between them was temporary, a momentary glitch in a perfect marriage in which he could do no wrong. God only knows what he would do if he discovered her true intentions. His words, *you'll be sorry,* replayed in her head, causing her heart to flutter. "I've got to go," she said.

Sam grumbled from underneath the pillow, then slid it down, revealing his face. Dayna kissed him on the forehead before running out the door.

By 4:00 that evening, Dayna was on the Mass Pike. She had left without Richard, assuming he would leave from the office and meet them at the restaurant. That was their standard plan whenever they had, in Richard's words, an early dinner. Her husband complained that anyone who ate dinner before 8:00 p.m. was still eating lunch. Dayna thought it was his way of denying he was a workaholic.

The Prudential Building came into view. Dayna took the next exit towards Copley Square where she merged onto Huntington Ave. She planned to cut through the city, making her way towards the South End where they were meeting Mark and Marilyn. Dayna wasn't surprised they'd chosen the South End. Since the 80's, the area had been run by yuppies who filled it with fancy restaurants, expensive condos, and tiny dogs. Outsiders often confused it with South Boston, more commonly known as Southie to the locals. Unlike the South End, Southie was famous for its rowdy Irishmen, zero parking, good beer and being home to the notorious Whitey Bulger.

She pulled up in front of the Atlantic Fish Company. It was one of those restaurants where you could get a nice "lobstah" and a bottle of wine that cost no less than sixty bucks. For Dayna, it was worth it just to have a valet and she handed her keys to the young man at the stand gratefully.

Inside, the hostess led her to a table towards the back of the room where Mark and Marilyn sat, two empty chairs across from them.

When Mark spotted her, he stood up, a big grin on his face. "There she is," he said, extending his arms for a hug.

"Here I am," Dayna responded with forced enthusiasm, succumbing to his embrace. His tailored suit scratched against her cheek.

"Hi, Marilyn," Dayna said, bending down to greet her with a light kiss on the cheek. Marilyn whispered a faint hello and continued to stare forwards. Dayna took the seat across from her, figuring Richard would want to sit across from Mark, his idol.

"Where's Richard?" Mark asked. His gaze drifted over Dayna's shoulder as if he suspected Richard might be hiding behind her.

She gave a careless shrug. "We always take separate cars. Richard usually leaves right from work if our engagements are any time before eight. He should be here any minute."

"Great. I can't wait to get myself a lobster," Mark said, rubbing his hands together. "So, what are you ladies drinking?"

Thirty minutes and three glasses of wine later, they decided to order food without Richard. When the smiling waitress came around, Dayna asked for the shrimp scampi. Mark ordered lobster for himself and halibut for Marilyn, who still stared eerily into the distance. The rose-pink dress she wore contrasted with her platinum hair, making her appear even paler than normal.

"I'm sure Richard will understand we needed to order food to soak up some of that alcohol," Mark said. "He'll be here soon. It's not like him to miss out on a good lobster."

"Perhaps he's just tied up at work," Marilyn said. Other than a few yeses and uh-ahs it was the first unsolicited comment she had offered all evening.

"I'm sure," Mark said. He patted Marilyn's slender hand. It seemed an odd gesture and Marilyn appeared oblivious to his touch.

Dayna felt sorry for them. All marriages had hidden problems and secrets, it seemed.

"It's really too bad," Mark began. "I had some big news for Richard." He paused and sipped his whiskey. "I suppose I can tell you now, Dayna. I mean why not? You can keep a secret, can't you?"

Oh, she could keep a secret all right. "Of course," she said.

"Well, as you know, Richard's been such a fantastic supporter of my fundraiser that I've decided he would make an excellent addition to the board. Greg agreed, of course, although he likes to stay behind the scenes. But Richard, he's the perfect fit. Not only is he well educated and respected in the field, but he has some great connections. Plus, I trust him with my life. He's one hell of a guy."

Dayna wanted to laugh aloud. "That's just great, Mark. I'm sure he'll be honored." Dayna wondered if the fake sincerity she'd forced into her voice sounded genuine. Mark smiled and she assumed it did.

A waiter returned with their entrees, followed by the wine steward who refilled their glasses. After the staff departed, Mark raised his whiskey and tipped his glass toward Dayna. "Richard's real lucky to have a wife like you, Dayna."

She half smiled.

"You know," Mark said, while tying his lobster bib securely around his neck, "I remember when Richard first told me he wanted to marry you. It was his second year of grad school. He showed up at my door one night with a few beers and asked me what I thought. He wanted to know how he could tell if it was the right time." Mark let out a little laugh. "At this point I'd been married to Marilyn here for almost seven years and I knew a thing or two about what it took to be married—and stay married." He smirked and squeezed Marilyn's hand again, a little too hard.

Marilyn did not react.

Mark removed his hand and cracked a lobster claw. Juices flew into the air. "I asked him if he loved you. He told me he did. That you made him feel like no woman had before. That you had an energy and honesty that was worth holding onto. And I told him, *'Then what the hell are you waiting for... marry the girl'.*" He paused to dip the meat into the cup of butter and pop it into his mouth. He swallowed. "Well, I suppose the rest is history. It just makes you feel old sometimes. That was what? Twenty years ago?"

"Twenty-six," Dayna responded. Tears were forming in her eyes. Not real tears, but the type of tears that glimmered in the right lighting so everyone around knew you were crying. It really was a sad story, she and Richard. But it wouldn't do her any good to go soft now. She took a sip of wine and held it in her mouth for a few seconds, feeling the acidity on her tongue.

She put down her glass, and brushed her lips with her napkin, then set it carefully beside her plate. Fixing her eyes on Mark, she asked, "Mark, you don't happen to know a Jessica Tate by chance?"

His glass paused on the way to his mouth. He seemed to take a few seconds to reset, then finished his sip and took his time replacing the glass on the table. "No, I can't say I do," he replied, following it with a little cough.

Liar. The guy couldn't even look her in the eyes.

"You know what?" he said. "If you would excuse me for a second, ladies. I'm just going to step outside and give that bastard a call." He rose from his chair while throwing Dayna a cheap grin and wink. He was still wearing his bib.

Dayna and Marilyn both watched him leave. Once he turned the corner and was out of sight Marilyn spoke. "Sorry if Mark seems a little on edge. He's just so preoccupied with the fundraiser that he sometimes forgets his manners."

Marilyn's giggle was so unnaturally quiet it sent a shiver down Dayna's spine.

"That's why I spend most of my time with the cats," Marilyn added. It was something most people would be embarrassed to admit or even utter, but she'd said it so proudly.

"Yes, the cats. I'm glad you have them," Dayna said and forced a smile.

"I don't know if you know the story, but Mark has a very personal connection to *Another Way*." Marilyn leaned in close enough that Dayna could smell the halibut on her breath. Marilyn dropped her voice to a whisper. "He treated Greg's sister, the one that killed herself. She took a bunch of pills, washed them down with vodka and tied a plastic bag around her head. Greg was the one to find Marlene, that was her name. Drove to her apartment in Woburn when his parents told him they hadn't heard from his sister in a few days. She had some issues, something they had to keep an eye on. Anyway, there was no note, but she'd left the song *Eleanor Rigby* on repeat. Greg called Mark after; it was a real mess. I guess that's why Mark started the fundraiser, he always felt… responsible." Marilyn said it with little emotion, as if she were simply reciting facts from a textbook.

Dayna wondered how many times she had related that story. How many times had Mark told it to her, trying to wrap his mind around why one of his patients would make such a final decision instead of seeking help? "Richard told me about it," Dayna said. "It's very sad."

"You have no idea just how sad," Marilyn acknowledged, an eerie film of water covering her eyes. "Richard was very upset when he found out about Marlene. Greg introduced them in college and the two became friendly, may have even dated if my memory serves me right. She was a very pretty girl, but like I said, she had some issues. Such a shame."

Dayna's heart fluttered at the mention of her husband's

name. "What sort of issues?" she asked, regretting the question immediately.

"Let me think. Mark doesn't like to talk about it much. I think it was Bipolar. No. No, that's not right." Marilyn began wringing her hands in a nervous fashion. "It was Borderline. Borderline Personality Disorder", Marilyn said with an emphatic nod. "I always get the two confused. I'm no psychologist, but I'm sure you are familiar with the disorder by now." She laughed again, that same creepy giggle.

Dayna felt no urge to laugh. Instead, her heart pounded in her chest so loudly she wondered if Marilyn could hear it.

"No answer," Mark said from behind her, catching them both off guard. Marilyn gave a squeak of surprise.

He resumed his position at the table, the lobster bib balled up in his hand. Marilyn shot him a worried look and began wringing her hands as if they were engaged in their own private war. It appeared she was back to her usual anxious self and Dayna realized, in the twenty something years she'd known Marilyn, Dayna had never heard her talk more than she had a moment ago.

"But I'm sure he'll show up any minute now," Mark added. He refastened his bib and shot an angry look at his wife.

Dayna nodded, but knew Richard wasn't going to show. Never had he been more than twenty minutes late to anything, never mind an hour. And he wasn't answering his cell. Richard always answered his phone; it was practically attached to him by an invisible umbilical cord.

He must be standing her up. Maybe he wanted to embarrass her as she'd done to him at the parties before. She experienced a stab of anger, but fought it down, reconsidering. Richard's absence didn't make sense. These were Richard's friends to impress, not hers. Plus, Mark was practically a father to him.

An image popped into her head of the call he'd received three nights ago during their fight. Richard had glanced anxiously at the ringing phone and taken a protective step in front of it. Dayna assumed he'd just been annoyed by the interruption, but likely he'd been trying to hide whoever had been calling, terrified she would see the caller ID flash onto the screen. Jessica, it had to have been.

Richard's words *you'll be sorry* echoed in her head. Maybe he had left her for good. What if he actually had the balls to trade her in for the new model? What better way to make his point than by standing her up in front of their friends. He'd take delight in making her look like the idiot who hadn't gotten the memo that their marriage was officially over. Another one of his manipulations designed to make her appear desperate and weak.

How foolish of her to think she could take the initiative. He had to be the one to leave her. It was probably his plan all along. She pictured the conversation he would have with Mark later... *Jeez, I'm sorry. I meant to call. I thought I made things clear when I said it wasn't going to work between us. That she'd gone too far by cheating. Showing up to dinner just must have been Dayna's way of holding on to our marriage. It's very sad, really. Did I mention she's been drinking a lot? Seeing things?*

Dayna stared solemnly down at her plate, looking at her food. She felt stupid. She wasn't special: Richard had tricked her just like he had those poor girls. Just like he'd probably manipulated Marlene. Was she his first? His first glimpse into the world of a Borderline? It may have been their relationship where he learned firsthand about the amazing, kinky and erotic sex he could get—but that was on a good day. On a bad day, she was really bad. Not quite right. Not quite sure who she really was. She may have even suffered from paranoid delusions and fears of abandonment.

Deep down, Richard was predictable, dull, and, to be honest, kind of lame. He lived a life of unimaginative monotony focused on his research and education. But the same personality that made him successful in his career couldn't handle the Dr. Jekyll and Mr. Hyde transformation of Marlene's disorder. Maybe that's why he married Dayna. For the stability and normalcy she brought to the table. Isn't that what Mark implied?

Dayna suspected he really loved her on some level. That he loved their son. But after a while it just wasn't enough to satisfy his deep hunger for the extreme and erotic. From her research, she'd learned BPD was a form of coping caused by family instability, neglect, sexual and/or physical abuse. Richard knew this and took advantage anyway. Even as a psychiatrist he continued to convince these girls into seeing him as their protector, the answer to all their dreams—their God. And when they didn't see him like that any more, he cast them aside. Is that why Marlene killed herself? Because of Richard? Suddenly, Dayna felt nauseous.

"Excuse me, I'm just going to run to the restroom," Dayna said, standing too abruptly, causing the silverware to rattle. She reached down to steady it and saw the dark woman—reflected in the shiny silver of the butter knife. When she looked back up, Marilyn was wringing her hands again. Dayna glared at her before turning and practically sprinting to the bathroom.

Chapter 26

The air freshener that was supposed to remind her of fresh linen only made her more nauseous. She ran to the closest bathroom stall and shut herself in, dry heaving once. She removed her cellphone from her purse and dialed Richard's number. It went straight to voicemail: *Hi you've reached Richard. I'm not able to take your call. Please leave a message and I'll get right back to you.*

Dayna ended the call before the beep and dry heaved a second time. The wall-mounted air freshener let out another puff of chemical fragrance. She redialed Richard's number getting his voicemail again: *...leave a message and I'll get right back to you.* Beep.

"I cannot believe you would do this to me, Richard. I don't know if you think this is some kind of joke, but it is not funny. And if you left me... you need to grow some balls and tell me to my face," she said in a whisper yell. "You better call me back the minute you get this. I swear to God!" If she could have slammed the phone down, she would have.

The bathroom door opened causing a bubble of panic to surface. Dayna froze, embarrassed she may have been overheard. She listened to the harsh clicking of heels on tile, then waited for the sound of a nearby stall to close before exiting her own.

Immediately, she was greeted by the figure. The crone. The dark woman. It stood across from her within the long mirror hung parallel to the row of sinks. Dayna considered running, the door was just a few feet from her left—but she didn't. Instead, she walked forward, choosing the sink directly in front of it and began washing her hands slow and deliberately. Surprised by her own boldness, she was completely calm, her pulse slow and steady.

"Back off," Dayna whispered.

The grey eyes poking from beneath the dark woman's hood

watched Dayna's every move.

Dayna shut off the water without breaking eye contact. A stall door closed behind her.

"Dayna," a timid voice said.

Dayna whirled around to find a pale Marilyn, who looked even smaller and almost hollow in the bathroom's fluorescent light. Her dress and shawl appeared to hang on her slender, skeletal frame.

When their eyes met, Marilyn began her infuriating hand wringing. "I see it, too," she said, her voice only a little higher than a whisper. "Just like I saw them that night."

"What?" Dayna asked, the tone of her voice rising to match Marilyn's. The brief moment of calm she'd just experienced slipping from her.

Instead of replying, Marilyn raised her thin hand and pointed. Dayna spun to face the mirror but found it empty. She pivoted back towards Marilyn only to find that she, too, had vanished. The heavy bathroom door still swinging shut from her exit.

Dayna did a slow turn, peeking under the line of stalls, then back to the empty mirror. Only her reflection, an incredulous look on its face, stared back at her. Had she imagined Marilyn, too? Clearly not: traces of her perfume hung in the air. The air freshener puffed again, dissipating the lingering evidence.

The nausea Dayna had managed to keep in check now threatened. She surveyed the bathroom one last time before escaping.

Back in the restaurant, Dayna snuck a cautious peek back at the table. Mark sat, bibbed, and preoccupied with his lobster. Marilyn, now back at his side, was staring into the distance, her face blank.

Unable to rejoin them and carry on as if nothing out of the ordinary had taken place, Dayna slipped out the front door. Hopefully, they would understand.

It was close to 7:00 p.m. when Dayna arrived home. The house was dark, with no signs of Richard. In the kitchen, she made another attempt to call him: ...*leave a message and I'll get right back to you.* Beep.

"Richard, pick up the fucking phone... please." She hung up, feeling defeated. Previous anger had given way to a state of anxious exhaustion. She began to pace, stopped, found a bottle of red wine and poured a glass. She studied it a moment—alcoholic blood in a glass—then dumped it down the sink.

She ran upstairs to Richard's room and flicked on the lights. Richard had left his room neat, not that she was surprised. He was one of those people who always cleaned up after themselves. He did it so well one might not even know he lived there at all. She opened his closet and a few of the dresser drawers. His clothes were undisturbed and folded. There was no sign he'd packed anything, no note saying he'd left.

She retreated, shutting the door, and walked down the hall to his office. She jiggled the door handle. Locked. Apparently, he was taking no more chances.

She tried knocking, the more appropriate first step. Maybe he'd forgotten about dinner and come straight home to work on his dissertation. "Richard?"

She banged on the door. "Richard?"

She shrugged. Had she really thought she would hear his chair push back from his desk or his footsteps as he approached the door: *Sorry about that honey, it wasn't my intention to be an inconsiderate asshole and stand everyone up at dinner.*

She bent to peer through the keyhole, an old 1920s touch they'd found charming and never updated. She could just make out the corner of his desk and his empty chair. She pressed her ear to the door one last time before giving up and retiring to her room.

She sat on the edge of her bed and scrolled through her phone until she found Greg's number. Composing herself, she dialed, hoping it wasn't too late to be calling.

Greg answered on the third ring. "Hello?"

"Hi, Greg, it's Dayna."

"Dayna, how are—"

"I'm sorry to bother you, but have you talked to Richard today?" She tried to take the anxiety out of her voice but must have sounded phony, like a waitress fishing for tips.

"No, I haven't heard from him in a few days. I actually need to run a few things by him now that I think of it. Is everything okay?"

"Yeah, everything's fine. I just—if you hear from him will you tell him to call me?"

"Sure. But Dayna—"

"Thanks, Greg. Have a good night."

Chapter 27

She was back in the wet place. It was humid and that same terrible smell, so strong it made her nostrils flare, hung stagnant in the air. A combination that smelled of burnt popcorn and decay.

Dayna still couldn't make out where she was. It was too dark. In the distance, though, she saw water, a small pond in the midst of total darkness, surrounded by tall cattails and ferns.

She advanced but did not want to see whatever lurked within the pond. The dread grew greater the closer she got. A ringing began, faint in the distance, growing louder with each step.

Dayna stood on the water's edge not wanting to look down when the ringing began again. Where could it possibly be coming from? She parted the cattails and leaned over the pond's edge, peering into the dark, murky water. The sound intensified. She clasped her hands over her ears. A grey hand shot out of the water, taking hold of her ankle. She screamed and leaned back. The hand pulled and she fell flat on her butt. She reached down, trying to pry the fingers loose. The nails were black, the skin rotting and slick with water. She wasn't strong enough. The hand dragged her forward. Desperately she grabbed for the cattails, but they slipped through her hands. Her feet were submerged in the water.

She was going to die.

She screamed, the air rushing from her lungs, but she could hardly hear herself over the deafening ring. With one big tug from the hand, she was under water...

She sat up in bed, drenched in a thick sweat. The ringing from her dreams persisted, then silenced.

The house phone, of course. Her head was still foggy from sleep and she struggled to find her cell phone somewhere on the far edge of the bed. She managed to hook it with her fingertips.

The screen was black, her battery dead. "Damn it," she

blurted, collapsing back against the pillow.

The house phone rang again.

The closest phone was locked in Richard's office and Dayna ran downstairs to the living room where a mock rotary telephone sat on an end table. She yanked the receiver up, dragging the base off the table.

"Hello?" she asked breathlessly, her chest heaving.

"Mom, it's me. I'm sorry to be calling so early."

"Max?" Her eyes found the clock on the mantel, 6:00 a.m. "It's okay. What's wrong? Is everything okay?"

"Is Dad there?"

"No, he's not. He's at work."

There was a long pause on the other end, so long she almost screamed at him.

"Mom, listen. I don't want to scare you, but we just received a call from McClain's. They're saying Dad hasn't shown up for work in three days. They didn't want to get the police involved but they're worried. He isn't answering his phone or responding to emails. They said that's very unlike him."

Her heart skipped a beat. She thought she might pass out and steadied herself on the arm of the couch. "Are you calling from work?"

"Yeah." He paused, perhaps waiting for her to go on but she didn't. "I told them I'd handle it, figured it was no big deal just a misunderstanding." When she still didn't say anything, he continued. "Is everything okay, Mom? Is he there now?"

"No, he's not. I already said that. I was under the impression he was at work, for Christ's sake."

"All right," he said, his voice taking on a more professional tone. "When was the last time you saw him? This morning? Last night?"

"Um." She had to pause and think. Spending nights with Sam, she'd come home late to a dark house or not at all. To be honest, she didn't think Richard had the balls to leave her until last night when he stood her up at dinner. "Maybe five days ago—Thursday."

"Jesus Christ. What do you mean you haven't seen him in five days? You didn't think to mention that to anybody? To me? What the fuck is going on?" The anger in his voice startled her.

"I—I don't know. We were supposed to have dinner last night with some friends, but he never showed."

"Jesus."

"I'm so sorry, honey. We've been having some problems. I..." She stopped, not sure what to say.

"Do you want to report him missing?" Max asked after a long pause. He was trying to sound calm, but she could hear the anxiety in his voice, the confusion.

"No," she said, her voice stern as if reprimanding a misbehaving child.

"No? What do you mean *no*?"

"I just don't think he's missing that's all. I think he left me."

Max's sigh echoed through the phone and vibrated in her ear. "I don't know what you're talking about or what problems you've been having with Dad, but either way I just think—I think it's weird he hasn't shown up for work, hasn't even bothered to call."

"Maybe work's not his first priority," she said spitefully, thinking of Jessica.

"Jesus. Well, if you're not going to do it, I will. Doesn't this seem strange to you? I get him not responding to *you*."

She cringed but let him go on.

"But, even if he did leave, why would he ignore me? His son."

She held her tongue. Maybe because he left to start a new fucking life with some unstable bimbo, she could have told him. For that matter, he may have even got her pregnant. Max's plaintive question finally penetrated her anger. "I don't know," she responded instead. "It wasn't about you, Max."

She heard him take a deep breath before replying.

"Well, to make things easier, I want you down at the Newton Police Station in an hour. I'll meet you there. You're his wife and the last person to see him, at least that we know of. We will call a few more people, but the cops will need you to answer some questions. I'm sorry, Mom. We'll find him."

"I'll be there."

"Oh, and one more thing, could you bring a recent picture of Dad?"

"Sure, honey," she said and hung up.

She frowned. How could Richard be so selfish? To put her and Max through this over some girl… it was ridiculous. And now the police were involved. If Richard ever had the nerve to show up back on her doorstep, begging for her to take him back, she'd squash him like the cockroach that he was.

Chapter 28

An hour later, Dayna walked up the stairs to the Newton Police station. Inside, the station was quiet. She searched the room for Max, but her eyes met those of a pinched-faced secretary hidden behind a plastic window instead. "Can I help you, ma'am?" she asked through the circular opening.

"Yes, I'm looking for my son, Max Harris."

"Oh yes, Mrs. Harris, right this way." The secretary stood, thumbing a button that released the door locks into the waiting room. The room was bare, with uncomfortable looking chairs and uncluttered coffee tables. With relief, Dayna followed the secretary through a second locked door.

Instead of taking her to Max, the woman led her to a back room where a few officers sat hunched at desks stacked with file folders and papers. Dayna recalled when Max initially wanted to join the force. One of Richard's cop friends had cautioned him that police work was 10 percent action and 90 percent paperwork. From the joyless expressions on the faces of these cops reviewing documents and typing lifelessly on keyboards, Dayna figured the guy's stats were probably accurate.

They made a beeline for a desk where a fit man with a sculptured face sat. Dayna placed him in his late thirties. He had the hardened look of a drill sergeant. He was leaning back in his chair so that the front legs hovered above the ground, his head angled down, reading what appeared to be a police report.

"Officer Brady, Mrs. Harris is here to see you," the secretary announced, as if the two had a pre-standing appointment to discuss flower arrangements for a party, not her missing husband.

Officer Brady glanced up, then returned his attention to the report. A few seconds ticked by and Dayna's irritation grew with each passing one.

"Ah, Mrs. Harris," he said finally, his chair thudding as it connected with the floor. He made a show of filing the report in a drawer, making it clear they were running on his time, not hers. "Officer Brady," he said, extending a calloused hand.

"Dayna Harris. But it seems you already know who I am," she said, taking his hand in hers. "Where's my—"

"This way please." He smiled a cold, toothless smile and ushered her down a bleak hallway. Pictures of officers and gold plaques decorated the walls. "Your son, Max, Boston PD, contacted me this morning regarding your husband, a... Richard Harris," he said, referencing the file in his hand.

"Yes I—"

"It appears your son has filed a missing person's report. He asked this be treated respectfully and locally. We aim to do both." The corners of his mouth twitched into a half smile.

They stopped outside a door labeled INTERVIEW 1. The door opened to reveal yet another room of white and grey, empty aside from a cheap, plastic table with opposing chairs. One wall was taken up by a mirror, certainly the infamous one-way mirror, and a camera was positioned in a corner near the ceiling.

Officer Brady ushered her to the table, as if she had a choice in the matter. "Please, have a seat."

She did as told. Despite the temperature, she shivered. The air had an uncomfortable, sterile feeling, similar to a hospital.

Dayna folded her arms across her chest and stared at the one-way mirror, wondering whether Max was on the other side, observing her. Officer Brady shuffled through more papers, apparently unconcerned with her comfort.

"My son told me he would be here. Where is—"

The door from the corridor opened. Max stepped through, handsome in his uniform. Dayna started to rise but hesitated when he made his way to the corner closest to the one-way mirror, where he stood with hands crossed in front of him, assuming the aura of the police officer Dayna saw so little of in everyday life. She stared at him, hoping he would acknowledge her. He didn't.

Officer Brady cleared his throat. "It appears we can begin."

"Max?" Dayna said, but received a tiny shake of the head.

"Mrs. Harris," Brady said, "I am going to ask you a few standard questions to help us get a better picture of your husband and where he might have gone."

Dayna rolled her eyes, but it appeared Officer Brady was too preoccupied with his papers to notice.

He tilted his head towards her. "Is that okay with you, ma'am?"

Dayna met his gaze, then stared at Max while uncrossing her arms and interlacing her fingers in front of her like a good student at her desk. She caught a glimpse of the injury on her wrist and pulled her shirtsleeve down to conceal it. "Sure," she said, trying to sound nonchalant.

"Okay. Please keep your answers short and concise. If questions can be answered with a 'yes' or 'no', please do so."

Dayna nodded.

Brady sorted the stack of papers with the intensity of a Wall Street businessman. He pulled one to the front and slid a legal pad next to him. "What is your relationship to the missing person, Richard Harris?" Brady held his pen ready, as if he didn't already know the answer to this question.

"He's my husband." She stifled the urge to add a big "duh" after the statement.

"And what is your husband's age?"

"Fifty-one."

"Approximate height and weight?"

"5'11. Maybe... 160 pounds."

"Eye and hair color?"

"Brown and brown."

"Does your husband have any mental or physical limitations?"

She stared at him. Hmm... he targets unstable women and manipulates them into having sex with him. Does that count as a "mental limitation"? "No," she replied.

"Does your husband have any identifying marks, such as tattoos or birthmarks?"

"No."

"Is it like your husband to miss work without giving notice or calling in?"

"No. He's a very hard worker. He has taken maybe three sick days in the past twenty years."

Brady shot her a look that she read as a reminder to keep the 'yes' or 'no' questions to 'yes' or 'no' answers. "Is it like your husband to not pick up his cell phone?"

"No."

"When was the last time you saw your husband, Mrs. Harris?"

She glanced anxiously at Max who stood rigid in the corner. He must have persuaded Brady to allow him in the interview room. The officer probably agreed on the condition that Max not interfere with the questioning.

"Five days ago, Thursday night." She swallowed, her throat dry.

If Officer Brady thought it was strange that so much time had passed, he gave no indication. "Where did you last see him?"

"At home. I got back a little after 10:00 that night. Richard was in the kitchen having a drink. We spoke for a few minutes and he told me he was going out. I fell asleep before he got home." Partly the truth, minus the argument. She wasn't sure why she was lying.

"Did he say where he was going?"

"No."

"And you didn't see or hear him return that night?"

"No. We sleep in separate rooms." Dayna studied Max when she said it. He, for the first time, returned her gaze with a troubled expression. "That's why I never heard him come

136

home. I just assumed he had gone to work the next morning like he always does. We've been having some... marital problems. Sleeping in separate rooms, avoiding each other, you know? That sort of thing."

"What was the cause of these marital problems?"

"Do I have to answer this?" Dayna asked, agitated.

"Could be important. Give us some insight into where he might have gone and why."

She took a deep breath. Her attention wandered to Max then settled back on the crow's feet radiating from the corners of Officer Brady's eyes. She wished Brady would ask Max to leave and spare him the details of his parents' crumbling marriage. She supposed she could ask Max herself, but he would just get mad. Besides, if he did leave now, he would only pester her later until he found out what she was keeping from him. "I walked in on my husband having an affair." She tried to say it clear and calm, but her throat was so dry. Did no one have the decency to offer her some goddamn water.

"When was this?"

"Maybe a month ago."

"Continue," Officer Brady prompted, making another scribbled notation on his legal pad.

"I came home unexpectedly one afternoon to find Richard in *our* bed with some blonde. Later, when I asked him about it, he told me the affair had been going on for a few years. I wanted to leave, but he promised he would end it and begged for forgiveness. I believed him, too, until I discovered he hadn't ended the affair and had been cheating on me for over ten years with at least four other girls. All of them patients." Her heart escalated to a steady thump. It was a shame Officer Brady was the first person she had told about the other girls.

"Girls?" Brady asked, eyebrows gathering in concern.

"Well, women I suppose. All maybe twenty-three."

Officer Brady nodded, making another notation.

"To me that's a girl," she added as an afterthought.

"Jesus," Max muttered from the corner and rubbed his face. Both Dayna and Brady looked at him, then back at each other.

"Were you or are you planning on filing for a divorce?"

"I'm meeting with a lawyer next week."

"Was this a mutual decision?"

Dayna shook her head. "Richard doesn't know. Initially, we both came to the decision that we would stay together. That it was for the best or at least easier. I mean, we've been married twenty-six years. My husband is well known in his field and has a reputation to uphold. Besides, I thought I could forgive him and that we could make it work... I really did." She paused and looked down at her hands. The white skin of her wound peaked from under her sleeve. "But I couldn't. I never said the words 'divorce', but since I found out about the other girls—women, I've been going out of my way to avoid him. I've been staying out late, I—"

"Staying out late?" Max asked from across the room, anger heavy in his voice.

Officer Brady whipped around in his chair and threw him a glaring look, clearly visible to Dayna in the mirror. Max shrank back into the corner, his mouth tightening into a thin line. Dayna hadn't wanted him to know any of this.

"I guess it doesn't really matter." She shrugged.

"And you're sure he never mentioned where he was going that night?"

"I'm sure. We had an argument and he left suddenly. I'm not even sure if that's when he went *missing*." She put the word in air quotes. "I hadn't even considered he'd actually leave me until last night when he stood me up at dinner."

"What makes you think he'd walk out on you? Leave?"

"That night, Thursday, Richard accused me of having an affair. When I admitted I was, he became irate and called me a whore and a hypocrite."

Max let out an uncomfortable sigh behind them but held his tongue.

"He also told me I'd be sorry, and he should just leave me, that I was the problem. So, I figured when he didn't show for dinner or answer my calls... he had. He's probably with that blonde right now on some island like they do in the movies." It came out more insensitive than Dayna meant, and she regretted saying it.

"So, he missed a prescheduled dinner last night? One you're sure he knew about?"

"Yes. He wrote it himself on the calendar. Richard's not the forgetful type."

"And you didn't think to report him missing or contact law enforcement?"

"Like I said, it wasn't unusual for us to go a few days without seeing each other. In fact, I preferred it. Plus, when you think your husband's left you, most people don't go running to the police. It's a private matter."

Brady looked at her skeptically. "Where were you that Thursday night, Mrs. Harris?"

"At home." Her heart fluttered. She felt attacked and scared. Everybody knew that was a question reserved for suspects... not victims.

"Is there anyone who can confirm that?"

"Yeah, my husband." Her tone was curt and unwavering.

Brady didn't respond, only scribbled away on his damn legal pad. It infuriated her. She leaned forward trying to see what he was writing, but he shifted the pad closer to him. Her pulse quickened; her face grew hot with anger. "This is unbelievable. You know that? Absolutely, unbelievable! You're making *me* into the bad guy here. My scumbag husband runs off with this girl he probably impregnated and you're asking *me* what I was doing on Thursday night. Why don't you call her? Huh?"

Brady looked up unfazed, as if dealing with lunatics was

an everyday occurrence. "We are just covering all the bases, exploring every angle. Standard." Bringing his attention back to the legal pad he noted a few more things. "Thank you for your time, Mrs. Harris. I'll just need you to write down a list of friends, family, or anyone you think your husband might contact or would know of his whereabouts." He flipped to a random spot in his pad, tore a page, and slid it across the table to her.

"I'll need a pen."

"Of course," he said, as if he were doing her the biggest favor in the world.

It must have rained while she was in the station. The sky was dark and a light mist still fell from the heavy clouds. She was halfway to her Chevy when Max called from behind her. She turned to find him jogging through the parking lot.

"Were you really just going to leave without talking to me?" he asked, his voice harsh and accusing.

Sometimes it was hard to believe he was that little boy she'd once held in her arms after he'd fallen off his bike, tearing the skin from his knee. With hot, wet tears spewing from his eyes onto her shoulder, he vowed he'd never ride his bike again. A promise he'd broken a few hours later after she convinced him to give the whole bike riding thing another go.

"You told me you were going to meet me here," she began. "I'm not even here two minutes before I'm ushered into that shitty little room with Officer Prick. I had no idea what I was walking into, Max. No idea. You didn't even look at me when you came in. You treated me like a criminal".

"Well, you didn't have to hightail it out of there."

"I did not hightail it out of there." But it was true. She really had blown out of the station after handing over her list of names to Officer Brady, slamming his pen back down in front of him. She had wanted to scream in his face and ask him why he was doing this to her, explain to him that with every second she spent dealing with this bullshit a little more of her spirit chipped away. But it wasn't just her who was being put through the wringer. It was a waste of Brady's time, too. Richard wasn't missing. Richard had left and didn't want to be found. Why couldn't anybody understand that?

She looked at Max, water droplets glistened in his dark hair. "I'm sorry, honey. I didn't want you to hear all that—to hear how shitty your parents' lives are." She let out a laugh of disbelief. "I tried so damn hard to keep it together, to sweep everything under the rug. To hide the truth from you, from myself, from everyone. I don't know. I just didn't think it would come to this, you know? That he'd leave and not tell anyone. I mean it's insane. How could he do this to us?"

Max pulled her into a snug embrace, his stubble rough on her ear. "I know. I know," he said.

Tears welled, then rolled down her face onto Max's crisp, black uniform. The scene wasn't much different from that day Max had crashed his bike, only this time she was the one crying.

Max held her until her sobbing ceased and the tears began to dry.

"They're going to work on the list of names you gave," he said. "Then, they'll send out a description to law enforcement across the country, check his credit cards, phone call history, that sort of thing. I'll let you know as soon as they find something." He pushed her back so he could look into her eyes. "They *will* find something."

"Okay, honey," she said, brushing an invisible strand of hair from his face. "Are you okay?"

He nodded. "I'm going to find him, Mom. Once I see that he's okay, then I'll kick his ass."

Dayna gave him a soft smile and kissed him gently on the cheek.

Chapter 29

Instead of heading home, Dayna went straight to Brookline Grille, where she now sat, nursing her second martini. It'd been just over an hour since she'd left the police station and her phone was ringing for the third time.

After receiving an irritated glance from a couple at the other end of the bar, she switched the phone to vibrate. It rattled on the bar top, then in her purse where she'd tossed it in frustration. The persistent phone was unnerving, much like the dark woman who had appeared in the mirror mounted behind the bar shortly after her arrival. At first the apparition had made her pulse flutter, but she got used to it.

Her phone vibrated. The couple glared at her again and she gave in, rummaging through her purse to find it.

The cell was blinking an angry blue with notification alerts. She clicked into them: fifteen missed calls, eight new voicemails. It appeared the police had made their calls to those she'd written on her list. She scrolled through the call log, scanning for Richard's name. Connie. Monica. Greg. Mark. But no Richard.

She dialed her voicemail and listened to the barrage of concerned messages.

Dayna, it's me... Dayna, just got a call from the police... Dayna, Richard's missing... Dayna, is everything okay... Asked me if I'd talked to him in the last five days... Where were you Thursday night... How's Max... Dayna pick up the phone... DAYNA?

Every message sounded the same, asked the same questions, relayed fake concern, until she came to the last one.

Max. Her heart skipped at the sound of his voice.

Hey, Mom, it's me. The guys contacted everyone on the list. No one's seen Dad in the last five days. The only person we couldn't get in contact with was Jessica Tate. Greg said she hasn't shown up for work in the last two days, but said she called in sick Monday morning.

They'll send a cruiser by her place later if they don't hear from her in the next twelve hours...

She stopped listening, unable to hear over the thumping of her heart. She glanced up at the mirror, to do a "can you believe this" sort of charade, but the dark woman was no longer there. Dayna was officially drinking alone.

Her phone vibrated again and she flung it at the wall. It fell short, hitting the floor, the battery popping out. A man at the other end of the bar rotated towards her, disgust showing in his face. She turned from him and regarded the approaching bartender. Either he was about to ask her to leave or cut her off. She held up a hand, slid off her stool, retrieved the phone and battery and left.

She wasn't drunk, but probably too buzzed to be cruising down Beacon Street at twilight. The dark woman had followed her. Dayna glimpsed her once in the rearview mirror. Then again in the windows of storefronts as she walked down Harvard Avenue, to Sam's apartment building. Maybe Dayna had been mistaken. Perhaps the dark woman wasn't the devil; she was her guardian angel.

"Jesus, Dayna," Sam remarked. "You started early today. I mean it's only six. You know people in Boston don't start blacking out 'til usually eight-thirty. Eight o'clock on a good day."

In no mood for jokes, she glared at him. His smile faded and he ushered her inside. He sat on the bed and patted beside him.

She stood a moment, considering, then tossed her coat on the end of the bed and began to pace. She told him everything. The affair. Richard leaving. The police interview. She told him about the other girls. She explained how Richard had targeted and manipulated them and how she'd discovered it all in his home office, hidden in plain fucking sight. It poured out in an intensity that surprised her. When she was done, she stood in front of him, breathing hard.

"Well?" she asked.

"I'm sorry for you," Sam replied.

She regarded him a moment, surprised to feel all the passion, energy and emotion drain away.

He patted the bed again. She lay down and Sam held her. He rubbed her back, kissed her cheek and promised everything would be okay. As their embrace lingered from seconds to minutes, his tender kisses became deeper and more urgent. His hand slid down her back to her ass. "God, I want you," he mumbled, before kissing her ear.

His hands travelled to the buttons of her pants where he struggled to unlatch each one. At the last button, he paused. "Do you want me to stop?" he whispered.

She shook her head. "No." She returned his kisses with more urgency, desperate to feel anything besides nothing.

They had sex with such intensity it made her cry out in pleasure and collapse when it was over. He folded her into his arms and she lay beside him, spent but fulfilled.

Chapter 30

The alcohol had worn off by the time she emerged from her short nap. The memory of the martinis lingered, leaving her with a nagging, full bladder. She wiggled out of Sam's embrace and made her way to the bathroom.

This time she shut the door. She peed, then washed her hands, not surprised to find the dark woman peering back at her from within the medicine cabinet mirror. Her grey eyes bulged from under her hood as she raised a wrinkled, dead hand to the glass, where she rested it delicately, like a child might do at an aquarium.

Dayna toweled off her hands while keeping a hesitant eye on the figure. The dark woman's hand banged against the glass, causing her to jump. The woman's eyes jutted from beneath the hood, the irises deepening to a dark, hateful grey. She continued to slam her hand against the mirror as if trying to escape.

The sound echoed in Dayna's head, her heart rate rising. She inched back towards the door. Another loud slam produced a thin crack in the glass. Dayna whipped around, fumbled for the door handle and retreated down the hall to the safety of Sam's room. He was on his bed, reading in the light of a small lamp clamped to the headboard.

She shut the door behind her and stood with her back to it, breathing hard. Faint echoes of the woman's pounding were still reaching her ears. She wondered if Sam could hear them, too.

He looked at her, closing his book. "Hey," he said. "How did you sleep?"

The knocking ceased. Dayna listened, eyes wide, waiting for it to resume. What if the woman got out? But that was stupid. How could she be inside a medicine cabinet in the first place?

"Dayna?"

She blinked and focused. His face radiated concern, but likely about her crazy behavior, not the knocking. She swallowed. "Yes?"

He tipped his head to the side, studying her a moment before replying. "I asked how you slept."

"I don't think I really did," she answered with a sigh.

"Me neither." He smirked. "Are you going to come back to bed?"

She scanned the room. The dark woman could be standing in any of the shadows. "Could we turn on the lights?" Dayna asked and without waiting for his response flicked the switch.

Sam shielded his eyes. "Yeah, sure." He chuckled. "Are you feeling any better?"

She took a tentative step toward him, glanced back at the still closed bedroom door. She settled on the edge of the bed. "Can I ask you something?"

"Sure."

"Do you believe in ghosts?" She felt silly asking and regretted turning on the light, allowing him to see what had to be a blush heating up her cheeks.

Sam scrunched his eyebrows. To her relief, he seemed to take the question seriously. "I suppose I do," he said.

"Have you ever seen one?"

"You know, I can't say I have." He rubbed his chin, as if searching his memory, then shrugged. "Don't get me wrong, I've had a few moments where I've heard something weird or seen something strange, but it was nothing I could ever confidently say was paranormal. I suppose we all have those moments where we freeze and are afraid to peer back over our shoulder, fearing what we might see. Classic kid's stuff."

He sat up fully in bed, then sipped from the bottle of Jack he'd left on his bedside table. He offered her the bottle, but she declined. He took another swig. "My grandma, on the other hand, would tell you differently. She swears up and down that ghosts are real." He let out a short exhale of a laugh. "She always told this one story. Get this... when she was maybe ten years old, my grandma used to see this little girl in the upstairs hallway of her house. Every night the little girl would be in the hallway, facing the back wall with her knees folded under her, slamming her forehead into the plaster over and over again. My grandma said sometimes the banging would even wake her up and she'd tiptoe into the hall and see her there, sure as shit."

Sam paused, peered into the bottle, then took another sip. "It didn't happen every time, but a few times the girl would stop banging, turn, and stare at my grandma, like she was angry she'd been interrupted. Granny said the eyes of the dead are not like mine or yours... where the whites are it's grey and where the color is supposed to be, it's just pure black."

Dayna thought of the dark woman and her grey eyes. Maybe Sam's grandmother was right. Maybe this figure Dayna kept seeing really was a ghost. "Do you believe her?"

"Dunno. She sure as hell believed it and no one wants to call their grandma a liar. To be honest, the stories used to scare the shit out of me as a kid. For a while, every time I got up to use the bathroom in the middle of the night, I was convinced I'd see that little girl at the end of the hallway, banging her head against the wall—but I never did." He laughed. "Why are you asking me about all this stuff anyway?"

"I don't know. Just curious."

"Curious about ghosts?"

"I don't know. It's just funny, that's all. I mean think about it. Let's just say there are twenty people at a party—"

"Sounds like a lame party," Sam interrupted.

Dayna flashed him a death stare, not amused by his immaturity. She cleared her throat and continued. "So, if you ask those twenty people how many of them have ever seen a ghost, I would venture to say that maybe eight or nine of them would raise their hands."

Sam nodded.

"Then, if you ask those same twenty people how many of them *know* someone who has seen a ghost, I'd bet nineteen of them would raise their hands."

Sam nodded again. "Yeah, sure. I would say that's probably true, but what's your point?"

"My point is a significant portion of the population has had some type of paranormal experience, but it's still regarded as taboo. Something people play off as being a trick of the mind or an illusion. A kind of scary, kind of silly, thing that people joke about on Halloween."

"Well, I think that's because for most people seeing a ghost or hearing footsteps is a one-time deal. It's nothing they can prove. It's just a fun story to tell over a few beers or whiskeys," he said, shaking the bottle of Jack.

Her eyes were becoming hot with tears. "But what if it's not just a one-time thing?" She paused. "What if—if it's a constant thing? A thing that's so unpredictable and scary that it drives you insane, wondering when or if you'll see it again."

His eyebrows furrowed. "What are you getting at?"

"Do you think ghosts can make you do things? Bad things?" she asked, tracing the outline of the scar on her left wrist.

"What do you mean? Like in the movies?"

She nodded.

Sam sighed. "Even if that was true, let's just say. I don't think ghosts can make you do anything you *really* don't want to. Everything else... it's just Hollywood, Dayna"

She swallowed.

He reached his hand out, resting it on her thigh. "What's up with you tonight? Is this about that girl you saw on the highway? Do you think she was a—"

"It's not important. I'm just tired. Let's go to bed."

He looked at her with a mix of concern and skepticism. It reminded her of the looks Scully gave Mulder on *The X-files*. He hopped out of bed and made a move for the lights.

"Can we sleep with the lights on?" she blurted as his hand hovered over the switch. "Just for tonight?"

His face said it all, but he dropped his hand and slipped back into bed nevertheless. He wrapped his arms around her. "No more thinking about ghosts tonight," he whispered into the back of her head, his breath tickling her neck.

"Okay," she muttered, but every time she shut her eyes, images of the dark woman floated through her mind.

Chapter 31

Knocking woke her, three quick raps.

Dayna jerked upright. The room appeared grey with only a thin line of sunshine sneaking in between the dark curtains. The left side of the bed was empty.

She rubbed her eyes, but the knocking sounded again. There was a short pause followed by three more raps. *For Christ's sake.*

She threw off the comforter and pulled on her clothes. Her eyes found the alarm clock: 7:30 a.m. Sam was up early. She poked her head out into the hall. She could hear the rush of the shower from the bathroom. Another three knocks came from the other direction.

She padded to the front door, and hesitated. Did she really want whoever was outside to see her in Sam's apartment? Of course, it was probably just the UPS man. No big deal. She rose on the balls of her feet and peered through the peep hole. Standing in the hallway, her back to Dayna, stood the dark woman.

Dayna gasped and stumbled backwards. This couldn't be happening. This entity... it wasn't real.

She eased her eye back up to the hole. The figure was still there and turned to face her.

Dayna bit her tongue to stifle a scream. What did this thing want? She stepped back, closed her eyes and pressed her palms to her forehead. This whole mess... these dark woman appearances were... were what? She dropped her hands and stared at the ceiling. She took a deep breath and blew it out. If the lady was a ghost, a spirit, then... images of Charles Dickens' ghosts in *A Christmas Carol* popped into her head. Why would a fucking ghost have to knock? Couldn't it go through the door? What was it doing, asking for permission to visit? *Can I trouble you for a cup of sugar, please? Certainly. Would you like to sit down on the sofa for a minute? Don't mind if I do.*

She snorted, awarding herself a grim laugh. Her subconscious was trying to tell her something by conjuring up all these images. But what?

She had to take control. She had to tell herself this thing was not real.

She took another deep breath, holding it until she was ready to breathe out. She turned to the peephole and looked out.

The dark woman was staring directly back, her grey eyes boring into her.

"Shit!" Dayna jumped back. "Shit, shit, shit!"

"Dayna?"

She spun to find Sam standing outside the bathroom door, a towel wrapped around his waist. "Something's outside," she said, her voice just above a whisper.

"Something?"

"Someone."

He padded down the hall, one hand clenching the towel. "Who is it?'

She just pointed, her hand trembling.

He looked through the peephole, then stepped back, opened the door, and peered out into the hallway.

Closing the door, he turned to her, his eyebrow raised. "Nobody's there, Dayna."

Sam made her sit on the bed and brought her a glass of cold water that she didn't drink. She hadn't spoken in five minutes. Sam dressed, every so often throwing her a worried glance.

This was it. After everything, *this* was her breaking point, the icing on the cake. She was too stressed, too broken. The dark woman wasn't real. Sam had confirmed that. And even if she was a ghost, well most people don't walk around seeing spirits in every mirror. She needed help; she could admit that now. She was sick. The dark woman could no longer be put off as something to deal with later or something that would fix itself on its own.

"I'm going home," she said and stood up.

"Dayna, what's going on? Tell me." He reached for her hands, but she batted him away. "Come on. What did you see in the hallway?"

"I..." She brought her hands to her temples and rubbed. "It's nothing."

"Sit back down; everything can wait. Just relax."

"No," she said, reaching for her purse and slinging it over her shoulder. "It can't wait."

The corners of his mouth turned down. "You're being rash."

A flicker of irritation bloomed, but she shook it off. How else could she expect him to react? She required help, probably needed to check herself into the looney bin. She couldn't allow him to stand in her way.

"I'm sick." She looked him in the eye. "And this, whatever this is between us... it can't work. You know that, right?"

"I know," Sam replied, a faint sadness in his voice.

"I'm not a happy woman. I haven't been for a while. You don't need this... any of it."

He moved for her hands again, this time successful in catching them. "You're happy when you're with me."

He said it with such conviction she could have hugged him. Instead, she shook her head. She was a sick woman and right now she was only his ball and chain. "Listen, I've been married to a man for twenty-six years that I didn't even really know. Now, he's missing. My son's out there searching for him and what am I doing?" She pulled her hands from his. "I'm here messing around with someone twenty-two years younger than me, almost the same age as my son. I'm a horrible person." She turned away.

"Come on. You're just stress—"

"I'm sorry, Sam," she said. "Stay away from me." *For your own good*, she wanted to add, but couldn't bear to look at him.

She muttered another quick sorry before running out the door.

She pulled into her driveway too fast for the incline and bottomed out. The underside of her car made a sickening bang as it connected with the pavement, rocking her forward in her seat. She threw the car in park, slammed her hands hard against the steering wheel, and yelled, "Dammit."

Overflowing with frustration, she sat for a moment, listening to the click of the engine as it cooled. A saying came to mind: God doesn't give you anything that you can't handle. Some well-wisher had told her that after the miscarriage. "Whenever a door closes, God opens a window," someone else said to her. Wasn't that from *The Sound of Music*? What a bunch of bullshit!

After the loss of her baby, she wasn't even sure she believed in God. For that matter, if there was a God, he must be some sort of sick bastard to make her suffer like this.

Her cellphone vibrated. Sam. It was his second time calling since she'd left. Either his heart was broken or he was worried about her or maybe a touch of both. She caught sight of the dark woman in her rearview mirror. She resisted the urge to look in the back seat. Been there, done that. If she turned to look, the old hag would be gone.

She sighed, got out of the car, and headed to the front door. "The thing isn't real," she muttered. "The thing isn't real."

Inside, Dayna turned to the front hall mirror that hung above the little table where she kept her keys and swung her purse at the glass. She thought of the famous film star, Greta Garbo, and how she kept a brick in her purse, swinging it at any paparazzi that dared approach her for a photo. She wished she had a brick now. The glass didn't break, and she was forced to take primitive measures. She dropped her purse and slammed her fist into the mirror. A crack zigzagged out from the target. She shook her hand, warm blood leaked from two of her knuckles. The pain felt good, refreshing. Alive. Stupid to use her hand, though.

She wandered into the kitchen and removed a carving knife from the rack, then used the butt to smash the upstairs hall mirror. She proceeded through the house, taking care of the rest of the mirrors.

She was being dumb, of course. She knew that. After all, she'd spotted the dark woman in other places than mirrors, but her aggressiveness was cathartic.

She ended in the master bedroom, starting with her vanity mirror. Her fist still stung from that first punch and blood trickled down her forearm.

The last mirror, above her dresser, was the biggest of them all. She stood before it, studying her own reflection. Behind her, the room was empty.

"Show yourself," she yelled. "Show yourself, you bitch."

She waited. If the dark woman appeared, what would that mean? That she was real? Dayna wasn't sure. She closed her eyes, counted to three and opened them.

The dark woman had come. She was standing behind Dayna's left shoulder. Her black hood up, her head tipped to one side as if puzzled, her eyes dark and brooding, the tiniest smile on her thin lips.

Dayna glanced down at the knife in her right hand. Perhaps now would be the time for one decisive act. Turn and slash. Would that kill the dark woman? What if she swung and the knife slipped right though her with no effect? Then what?

The knife felt strangely light in her hand, easy to use. She must have cut herself again, perhaps on the blade when she'd clobbered the other mirrors, because blood was streaming from her palm, coating her wrist and dripping on the white rug beneath her feet. Dayna stared at her bloody wrist and an image surfaced, another use for the knife that would fix everything. One quick slash and it could all be over.

She shivered and dropped the deadly weapon.

Behind her, the dark woman smiled. *Bitch!* Dayna picked up

a crystal vase on the corner of her dresser, filled with water and a bouquet of faded red roses from before Richard had brought his mistress into their house, and hurled it at the glass.

The vase and mirror exploded. Water, flowers and shards of glass showered the dresser.

The dark woman vanished, and Dayna laughed.

Chapter 32

Dayna paused at the top of the stairs, throwing a glance over her shoulder. A fresh trail of blood created by tiny droplets began at the door to the master bedroom and ended by her feet. She continued down the stairs, the blood following her, marking every few steps. In the kitchen, she tore a paper towel from the holder, wrapping it sloppily around her wounds and stood over her dead cell phone.

She struggled to find her charger and fought her shaking hands to insert the plug into her phone. After a few seconds, the cell was revived, greeting her with a glaring blast of blue light. It took a moment for the notifications to load. Those who had tried calling her relentlessly last night must have given up and only missed calls from Sam and Max were displayed.

As her finger hovered over the screen, the house phone started ringing, echoing from the living room. Dayna dropped her cell and ran to it.

"Mom, I've been trying to get in touch with you all morning." It was Max. "Where have you been?"

"Sorry, I—"

"The cruisers went by Jessica's house this morning. They said she was in real bad shape, hair a mess, hadn't showered in a while. She claimed she hasn't heard from Dad in five days... well, I suppose six now. She said she'd tried calling him, but it kept going straight to voicemail. She's worried."

Dayna lowered the phone. Jessica was worried? How kind of this girl to be worried about *her* husband. Dayna's cheeks flushed with anger. She lifted the phone back to her ear. Max was rambling on. "And they believe her?" she interrupted.

"What?"

"I said, and they believe her?"

There was a moment of silence before Max answered. "Of

course there's a chance she could be lying, maybe covering for him, but the guys don't seem to think so. Brady spoke to her himself. She was really broken up about it. She said he would never just leave her like this."

How ironic! Dayna had thought the same thing herself. She felt like throwing the phone. "Well, I just don't know, Max. I don't know where he is..." She trailed off, unsure what to say. As she stared at her feet, another drop of blood materialized on the wooden floor.

"I'm going to need that picture, Mom. You forgot to bring it yesterday. I was hoping we'd have a lead by now and wouldn't need it, but—"

"Shit. I totally forgot."

"I'll send some guys by in twenty minutes to pick it up."

Perfect! Just in time for them to see the trail of blood throughout the house, the smashed mirrors. "It's okay, I'll run it down there this evening. It's no trouble."

"Well... I thought I'd have them check the house, too. Maybe do a quick walkthrough."

Her heart leaped. "No!"

"Huh?" he said.

"Do you really think I'm that stupid and haven't checked my own house? What do you think? All this time he's been hiding in the closet?"

A sigh, then, "That's not what I think, Mom. This Jessica girl, she's got a history... she could be dangerous. Now that we've questioned her, she might come to see you. Accuse you of something."

"I'm not a child, Max. I can take care of myself."

He sighed again in defeat. "All right. I want that picture ASAP. I'll check in with you later and for God's sake keep your fucking phone on."

Her assignment from Max had her retracing her steps,

following the blood and her path of destruction back upstairs to her bedroom.

She needed to stand on tiptoes to reach the few photo albums she'd stored on the top shelf of her closet. The first album contained the most recent photos, although few had been added in the last ten years or so. With Max grown up, the camera had been retired.

She placed the album on the bed and opened to a picture of her and Max on his graduation day from the police academy. He stood in his uniform, a foot taller than her, a beaming smile on his face. She and Richard had been so proud of him, treating Max to a prime cut of steak from one of the best grills in Boston later that day.

When she flipped to the next page, to her photo of Richard and Max at the ceremony, she gasped. Richard's face had been scribbled over in what looked like black sharpie. On the facing page was another picture of her and Richard, his face—again—covered by black marker.

Confusion washed over her as she paged through the rest of the album. Angry black scribbles desecrated each photo of Richard.

Her heart accelerated. Max was right. Maybe Jessica was dangerous. Maybe she had snuck into their house in a rage, defacing the man who had betrayed her. But that didn't feel right. Wouldn't it make more sense for Dayna's face to be blacked out? Maybe Jessica would prefer to be the woman in the photographs, the wife of a successful psychiatrist instead of just the mistress. Besides, how would she even know the albums were in the closet?

Dayna clutched at her stomach, sure she was going to vomit. She could barely take care of one problem before another unfolded. What the fuck was going on? She should call Max and let him know about the defaced photos; it could be a clue. But the thought of Jessica creeping through her house caused a shiver to travel up her spine. She had to get out of there.

She ran downstairs and out to her car. As she put her Chevy into reverse, the thought came to her—she knew exactly whom she needed to talk to and where she was going to go for answers.

Chapter 33

It was just after 1:00 p.m. when she came to a screeching halt in front of the big, white house. Yesterday's rain had persisted through most of the morning and the sky was still overcast. The air was cool and crisp, more reminiscent of fall than early May.

Dayna sprinted to the house and banged on the door. After a dozen knocks, it opened, and she halted, her fist nearly colliding with the small figure on the other side.

Marilyn stood ghostly pale in a light-blue bathrobe, a grey cat wrapped in her arms. With no makeup, the dark circles under her eyes were even more prominent, making her look frightened and old.

"Dayna! What are you doing here?"

"Where's Richard?" Dayna demanded.

"You shouldn't be here," Marilyn said, her voice dropping to a whisper, her hands clutching the cat. "You need to leave."

Dayna ignored her. "I know you know something. What did you see, Marilyn? What were you trying to tell me in the bathroom?"

"You shouldn't be here," Marilyn said again. She peered over her shoulder, then turned back to Dayna. "You need to leave."

As fast as Marilyn stepped back, Dayna stepped forward, jutting her foot into the house, stopping the door from closing. "I'll rip that fucking cat from your hands, Marilyn. I swear to God."

Marilyn pulled the cat closer. "I know what they did," she said. Marilyn began petting the cat with furious intensity.

Dayna felt her pulse quicken in her neck. "Tell me."

"It was 2:00 a.m. when the house phone rang," Marilyn said, just above a whisper. "Mark picked up like he'd been expecting it. He said there was an emergency at McClain's and he'd be back in an hour. But I knew... I knew something wasn't right."

Marilyn's eyes glazed over, as might a dementia patient lost in distance memories. "After he left, I peeked out the window and I saw *him* with Mark."

"Who?" Dayna asked, edging forward. "Who did you see?"

"Richard. He was by his car, arguing with Mark. I couldn't hear what they were saying, but after a while they stopped talking. Richard opened the door to the back seat and began pulling something out. It seemed heavy. Mark came around the side and took the other end. It was dark, but..." Marilyn's lips quivered. "It was Marlene. I'd recognize that red hair anywhere. They carried her to the back of the car. As they lifted her into the trunk, her head rolled back in this awful way and I screamed."

A tear rolled down the side of Marilyn's cheek. The cat struggled in her arms, but she held him tighter. "Mark looked up and saw me in the window just before they drove away with her. I... I was so scared."

Marilyn stopped.

Dayna gripped her hand, lifting it away from the cat. "Then what, Marilyn? Where did they go?"

"I don't know where they went." Marilyn closed her eyes and shuddered.

Dayna gave her hand a forceful shake. The cat shifted. Marilyn opened her eyes and wrenched her hand free, clamping it over the cat's upper back.

Marilyn sighed. "All I know is the next day, Greg found his sister with a plastic bag over her head. The police said Marlene had drugs and alcohol in her bloodstream. When Mark came home he never said anything about it, about him seeing me at the window, I mean. But the way he looked at me..." She shuddered again. "I knew... I just knew he'd kill me if I uttered a word. I could never leave. I could never leave," Marilyn whispered over and over again as she stared into the front yard, petting the cat with tears spewing from her eyes.

Dayna's heart was pounding, thudding against her ribs.

"Your husband's not who everyone thinks he is, Dayna. He has an appetite and I think Mark feeds it. He's more than just his mentor... he's his inspiration."

"What are you talking about?"

"I've found things—pictures. I know you have, too. I could see it in your eyes that day at the restaurant." She turned to Dayna and stiffened. "You've changed, Dayna. There's a darkness in you now. I only know because it's in me, too."

"Marilyn!" Mark called from somewhere in the depths of the house.

Marilyn let the cat fall from her hands, her eyes wide. She grabbed Dayna's arm. "Marlene... the poor girl wasn't right. I think... I think something happened. She broke it off with Richard and he couldn't handle it." Her whispers came out scared and urgent.

"Marilyn!"

She looked over her shoulder then back to Dayna. "If he did that to her, did you really think that he'd let you leave?"

"For Christ's sake, Marilyn, where's dinner?" Mark yelled.

"You need to leave now," Marilyn said.

Something twigged in Dayna, something she had to find out. "What about the woman in the glass, Marilyn. Do you see her, too?"

"You need to leave," Marilyn said again before slamming the door in Dayna's face.

Chapter 34

A cat meowed behind her. Dayna spun towards the soft purring. The cat approached and rubbed against her legs. She bent to give it a scratch behind the ears.

Mark's footsteps echoed from somewhere in the house. Dayna jumped up and hustled down the walk. Best not to let him find her here.

She hopped in the Chevy, imagining a killer on her tail. She gave a quick look toward the house and saw nobody, but the imperative to get away was just as strong. The tires screeched as she pulled away from the curb.

Now she understood everything. Mark hadn't started the fundraiser because he felt guilty. He started the fundraiser because it would lift the attention off him. After all, how could such a kind, generous man possibly be an accomplice to her husband's crime?

And Richard. How could Richard take a life? According to Marilyn, not only was he a pervert, he was a killer.

She was back at her house in under twenty minutes, bounding up the stairs two at a time. She needed to gather her things, pack a suitcase, and get the fuck out of the house before Richard decided to come back and make his grand reappearance. She'd be stupid to sit around and wait. She'd get a hotel room, call Max once she was safe, and tell him *everything*. Then, hopefully, Richard would rot in prison where he belonged, right next to the other murderers and sexual deviants.

In the upstairs hall, she froze outside Richard's office door. How could he rot in prison if there was no proof? Would the police even take her seriously without it? There was no way she could get him on a twenty-year-old crime, even if it was murder—it was a little too late for that. But naked photos of his patients could rile things up. She was foolish not to take them when she'd had the chance. No way in hell the police would listen to her without them. After all, how convenient for her to accuse her husband of murder when she was the top suspect in his disappearance.

She turned towards the office door and wiggled the knob. The door was obviously still locked. She kicked as hard as she could. It took four tries before the lock finally gave out under her weight and the door swung open.

The office was empty and eerily undisturbed. Dayna searched the desk again, although she knew it was probably pointless. No way Richard would've put the photos back after he'd already moved them... but she had to be sure.

She pulled open the bottom filing cabinet but found no gold stars or Polaroids. The only place left to look was the oak bookshelf tucked in the back corner of the room. It was tall, standing maybe two feet over her head, filled with books on psychiatry and medicine. As she approached, the air conditioning kicked on, startling her. It was the first few days of May, but Richard always liked the house cool.

The vent blew a blast of cold air into her face from above. For a moment, she thought she smelled burning. Where was that coming from? She peered up at the vent, then, out of the corner of her eye noticed a glimmer of blue hanging—just barely—off the edge of the bookshelf's uppermost shelf. Whatever it was had been stored sloppily, Richard didn't do sloppy, he did meticulously neat.

She rose onto the balls of her feet and reached up, her fingers flirting with the edge of what felt like a cardboard box. A little more of a stretch and she was able to nudge the box to the edge. It was so damn close. She jumped and slapped the side of the box, knocking it from the shelf. She made a desperate effort at a catch, but it slipped through her sweaty palms. The box hit the floor on an angle. The cover popped off and the stack of

Polaroids slid out.

She'd found them! Richard couldn't bear to throw them away. She kneeled, gathering the scattered photos into her hand. She shuffled through them, finding the four she'd already seen along with an additional eight. The new photos were of the same girls in different poses and various places. Each picture caused her stomach to tighten, but the last one was the worst. It depicted Jessica, posed naked, in *their* bed. The bed where she and Richard had slept, read books, and, at one point, even made love.

She rested the photos by her knee and righted the box. Inside were newspaper clippings. The first clipping was Marlene's obituary from 1990, documenting her brief life and declaring her death 'unexpected' after a long emotional battle. The second was the obituary of Audrey King, twenty-three, death also described as unexpected. The last, a Sandra Hill, was more of the same.

The clippings shook in her hands. Richard had held onto the obituaries. Just like the pictures—the clippings were trophies.

She shuffled through the clippings, staring at the women's faces. Pretty girls whose lives had been cut short by her husband, maybe by Mark, but either way Richard was involved. Isn't that what Marilyn had implied? Why had Richard killed these three women? Had they threatened to ruin his career when he broke it off? If he could do this to them, what would he do to her?

She collected the evidence and stood up. The AC vent blasted her in the face a second time. The cool air felt good, but the rank smell of burning hit her again. It was vaguely familiar, reminiscent of the ripe smell of her dreams. The thought hit her that the house might be on fire, but she shook it off. Burnt toast, maybe, but not like a wood fire.

She pivoted towards the adjoining bathroom. One of Richard's favorite touches. God forbid he stop working for even a few seconds to walk down the hall to relieve his bladder. Was that where the smell was coming from? Maybe stirred up and carried by the AC vents? One hand rested on the handle of the bathroom door, the other grasped the Polaroid's with fierce intensity. There was a sinking feeling in her gut. She should be packing, needed to be packing, but something was pushing her forward, urging her to look in the bathroom.

She swung the door open and the smell hit her immediately. It wasn't just the same burnt smell from the vents, but a new and powerful odor, like nothing she'd ever smelled before. It was almost enough to make her leave the room and shut the door behind her.

Holding her nose, she walked to the toilet and lifted the lid. The water was clean.

She turned and screamed. The dark woman hovered above the tub, pointing down. In the water was Richard, his eyes wide and unblinking, his pupils turned up, almost lost behind his eyelids. The skin on his face and upper chest was a ghostly white and wrinkled. His radio, usually on his office desk, bobbed between his legs in the murky, discolored water. Dayna's eyes followed the cord to the wall outlet where the radio was still plugged in. The plug looked charred, the rubber peeling.

Dayna sank to her knees. She looked up at the dark woman. "What have you done?" Dayna screamed at her. "What have you done?"

The dark woman extended her hand, aiming a finger toward Dayna. "You," the dark woman croaked.

The word echoed in Dayna's head, banging off the inside walls of her skull, slicing through her mind.

"Remember," commanded the dark woman.

"No," Dayna said again. "I don't want to."

"Remember."

Unbidden fragments of images tickled her mind, like the tidbits of a dream that linger after one awakens, just out of reach. Almost against her will, she fought to retrieve them. An argument with Richard. Whiskey on his breath. Whore! Yes, he'd called her a whore. A slap? He'd slapped her? No. There was no slap. He had caught her wrist.

He had left in his Porsche while she'd retreated to the bedroom, tired and defeated.

Something had happened, then... something terrible. She opened her eyes wide.

"Yes," hissed the dark woman.

She was in her bedroom. She had just pulled her silk pajama dress over her head when she heard the unmistakable hum of the Porsche's engine. Headlights illuminated the bedroom, followed by a bang. She ran over to the window and peered out through the curtains. Richard must have hit the back wall of the garage, he was probably too drunk to drive. He must have decided to come home...

Dayna was back on the cold tiled floor of the bathroom, four feet from her dead, bloated husband. She couldn't bear to look at him, didn't want to see his glassy, dead eyes. She squeezed her own shut...

Her heart pounded. She ran to grab her robe from the back of the door and pulled it snuggly around her. The front door slammed. Footsteps on the stairs. Then, silence. He was standing outside the bedroom door. She moved for the dresser, pretending to busy herself.

"Dayna?"

Her body went rigid.

"I know you're in there," he called again.

The bedroom door slammed open...

Chapter 35

Slam.

Dayna whirled around, pulling her bathrobe tighter. A disheveled Richard was leaning against the door frame, his shirt unbuttoned, the blue tie she had given him for his fiftieth birthday, loosened and askew.

"Dayna," he said, advancing towards her.

He knocked the black scarf concealing her vanity mirror carelessly to the floor as he brushed past. It didn't take much for her to see he was piss drunk. He had probably polished off the rest of the Crown Royale in the car before deciding to turn around and come home. The smell of whiskey radiating off him was sickening. He reached out and took her hands.

"What do you want, Richard?" she asked, slipping her hands free from his limp grasp.

"I want you. I miss you." He paused. "I was just thinking... let's just forget about the fight, forget about everything." He inched closer, placing his hands on her waist.

She wriggled free and edged backwards. "You're drunk. You don't know what you're saying."

"Jesus. Get off your high horse, Dayna. I'm just having a little fun. You drink all the time. I'm not the one who's delusional here."

Her heart thudded. Did he know about the dark woman? Had she told him? She couldn't remember.

"Finding so-called incriminating pictures that were never there and accusing your husband of things he didn't do... grow up." He laughed.

She wanted to call him a liar, but his tone frightened her. She ignored him and busied herself with the dresser again, pretending to search for something in the drawer.

He took a slurred, but softer tone. "Listen, honey, I'm sorry. I didn't mean that. I just miss you, that's all. You're still my wife and

I'm trying here. I really am." He paused, rubbing his forehead. "But I have needs, Dayna. Real needs."

His voice sent a shiver up her spine.

"I'm tired, Richard. Go to bed." She continued to riffle through the drawer. She did not want to deal with this: not tonight—not ever. She just needed to make it to next week. Her appointment with the divorce lawyer was on Friday.

"Come on, sweetheart. Don't be such a prude." He grabbed her arm, twisting her around to face him and pulled her close. His boner poked through his slacks. "You can't go around looking like that and not expect me to get excited. You know I love that silk nightgown." He kissed her neck, his breath hot and sour.

His left hand held her arm in a vice-like grip. He placed his other hand on her breast. "You're so beautiful."

"I want you to leave," she said, straining against him. "You're hurting me."

"I'm not leaving."

She turned her head, trying to escape his lips and the overpowering scent of whiskey. "Stop it, Richard. You're disgusting."

"I'm disgusting? You think I'm disgusting?" He shook her. "Well, I think you're a whore. The biggest bitch I've ever known. I've stopped the affair and what do you do? You go and have an affair yourself, then act like you're better than me. Hah! You'll let someone else touch you but have the nerve to deny your own husband. What you need, my dear, is a good fuck—"

She slapped him so hard it stung her hand. Richard stared at her, his eyes wide. He lunged forward, grabbed her by the hair and dragged her towards the bed. She screamed, grappling for his wrist. She managed to get a grip on his hand. She bent her knees, trying to get purchase with her toes. He yanked harder and she screamed again.

"Please, Richard. You're hurting me. Let go."

He bent her over the bed, slamming her head into the mattress, and held her in place with one hand as he unzipped his pants with the other.

"Please," she cried again, sobbing.

His grip lessened. She tried to move, to turn around and kick him, but he was too fast. With both hands, he ripped down her underwear, then pinned her down with a rough hand on the back of her neck.

"Richard, no!" she blurted, struggling to avoid being smothered against the bed.

He entered her. She screeched at the sudden, tearing jab, paralyzed by the pain. He eased back, then drove in harder. She tried to relax: anything to stop the fire. Defeated and broken, she moaned, sobbing with each thrust, one after another, each accompanied by a vile grunt from Richard.

He paused once to lift her silk nightdress higher. She prayed that it was over, that the alcohol would prevent him from finishing. Instead, he spit on her and shoved himself into her ass. She cried out in pain and anger.

"Is this what you like? Uh?" he whispered, his lips brushing her neck, his tie caressing her upper back.

"F-f-fuck you," she squeezed out.

He laughed, and for a moment, held still. "If you insist," he said, and began thrusting again.

She hated him! She wailed for herself... for the other girls... for her son.

She squirmed beneath him, gasping for air. She was able to turn her head enough to get a breath.

There she was. The dark woman loomed within the vanity's exposed mirror

Their eyes met, and Dayna felt a sudden, new connection. Help me, Dayna mouthed.

Richard yanked her by the hair again, craning her neck back at an unnatural angle. She reached up and batted at his hand, as much to maintain eye-contact with the dark woman as to relieve the new pain.

"This is what you deserve," he said, leaning down, pressing his mouth firmly against her ear. "You whore."

He shuddered and groaned, pressing deep into her, then withdrew and slammed her against the bed. Finished.

Chapter 36

She curled into fetal position and listened to his breathing. He grunted, then gave a little, familiar groan. Dayna pictured him leaning back, hands behind the small of his back, stretching out the kinks. She heard him shuffle across the floor and pull open one of the dresser drawers she still allowed him to keep a few items in, all while he was whistling — incredible! Whistling just above a whisper, like he often did when moseying around. Business as usual.

He left the room and made his way down the hall. She heard the office door's hinge squeak, then the door to the attached bathroom swing open, followed by the sound of water: not the sharp splatter of the shower but the gush of water falling into the bathtub. A soft tinkle of music sifted from the bathroom and floated down the hall. He must have moved the radio he kept on his desk into the bathroom. It was probably above him on the windowsill. How quaint.

Wincing, she rolled over onto her back. She swung her legs to the edge of the bed and pushed herself up on her elbows. She paused, gathering her strength before finally sitting up. She put a hand behind her neck, wincing as she tipped it from side to side.

She looked at the phone on the night table, studying it a moment. She should call the police. She hadn't showered; they could easily do a rape kit. Marital rape was a crime. Her ass was sore. It was probably bloody, which would show aggression.

However, the thought of sitting in the witness stand staring at Richard's smug face made her want to puke. Not to mention she'd be known for the rest of her life as the poor woman who got raped by her husband, the famous psychiatrist. People would be whispering behind her back that she was a liar, an angry bitch who wanted more money in the divorce settlement. Or worst of all, that she brought it on herself. After all, rape doesn't apply to married people. How could it?

His word against hers — as always.

She got to her feet and tottered, gritting her teeth against the stabbing pain. She hobbled down the hall and paused outside the office door, listening to the soft hum of music. It sounded like The Beatles, maybe Eleanor Rigby.

She needed to see him in there, glimpse him relaxing in the tub, prove to herself that her husband of twenty-six years really was a sociopathic asshole.

The office was empty, barely lit by the dim glow of the antique desk lamp. Another half-filled bottle of Crown Royal rested on the desk, next to the crystal battleship paperweight she had gifted him. She had the sudden urge to slam it to the floor. That stupid thing had cost her almost $100, a ridiculous sum of money to feed into Richard's boyhood fantasy of manning a war ship. He didn't deserve it then and he certainly didn't deserve it now.

Her eyes moved to the ajar bathroom door. She stepped inside. Richard lay in the hot tub. Steam rose from the water, swirling before dissipating into the air. His head was reclined back against the porcelain, his eyes closed, his lips formed in a small smile. Enjoying post-coital relaxation.

He cracked open his eyes. "What are you doing in here?"

She froze. What was she doing in here? Suddenly her plan of peeking in on him seemed ludicrous.

"Do you want to get in here with me?" he asked, grinning.

"Are you kidding?"

"Come on," he said.

She clenched her jaw, resisting the urge to scream at him. "I could press charges," she began, but stopped when he laughed.

He raised his arms, linking fingers, and placed his hands behind his neck. "You've already decided not to," he said, "or you wouldn't be in here with me now."

She closed her eyes. The guy could read her like a book. He knew her so well, certain that he had her under his thumb.

"I know you, Dayna. You're too proud. You will sweep it under the rug like you always do, like you should do. Besides, a whore like you deserved everything I gave you."

Her head felt hollow and a heat spread through her entire body. Her eyes scanned the room, steadying on the radio nestled on the windowsill above the tub. She scooped it up, raising it above her head.

Richard's brow furrowed. "What are you doing?

She took a step forward and his eyes widened. "Put that down!"

It was his turn to beg.

His gaze darted towards the door. "Please, Dayna." He propped his elbows on the sides of the tub, struggling to push himself up. His feet slid beneath him as he desperately tried to get a grip on the slippery porcelain. He fell back, his face submerging. He struggled, his limbs flailing in terror, then resurfaced. His eyes were shut. He opened them and met her gaze. "Please," he said again.

She let the radio fall.

It landed on top of him with a splash. The outlet sparked and let out an audible crack. His arms dropped from the sides of the tub as his body convulsed. Water pooled onto the floor.

She took two steps back, but her eyes never left Richard's.

His body went still.

Dayna stared into his dead eyes for what felt like a long time. A shadow flitted across the porcelain tiles above him and she whirled around. The mirror was empty.

She turned back and gasped. The dark lady was in front of her and she was smiling.

Chapter 37

Back in the cold, empty, tiled bathroom, Dayna was left with a brief flashback of herself standing above her bed, the photo albums spread out as she blackened out the face of the man who'd once been her husband. She blinked, and the vision faded. Her heart pounded. What had she done?

She was a *murderer*.

Her stomach clenched hard. She pulled herself onto unsteady feet and bolted for the toilet. She knelt before it, staring into the clear water, but nothing came up. She took a deep breath and exhaled slowly, her fingers still gripping the toilet's porcelain rim.

She had killed her husband.

This time it was a little easier to admit and her heart didn't pound quiet so hard. Yes, she had killed him: electrocuted him with his own radio and stuck around for the show. She'd watched as he convulsed and the water darkened from his bowels letting go.

She lifted her head, releasing her death grip on the rim, and stood. She moved for the sink, averting her eyes from the body in the tub. She lathered soap between her palms, wondering if they'd ever feel clean again or if the dirtiness would remain. Could she live with what she'd done?

She turned off the faucet and looked into the mirror. The dark woman peered back, but this time she blocked Dayna's own reflection. Dayna cocked her head to the side, raised her hand and let it fall—the dark woman did the same. Bracing herself on the sink's edge, Dayna leaned forward, bringing her face an inch from the glass. As she stared into the dark woman's eyes, Dayna realized they were her own. Her heart fluttered. Had she really been that stupid? Was it possible that all this time she'd been running from this... this... dark phantom, she'd just been running from herself, the darkness inside her. The thought was almost ludicrous and Dayna smiled. The dark woman smiled back.

A new energy overcame her. Worries about being able to live with her murderous act evaporated. She felt empowered and a strange sense of freedom washed over her.

She exited the bathroom, closing the door on her dead husband, whose path of destruction and lies were laid out before him in scattered Polaroids and newspaper clippings. Hopefully, they'd form a trail back to Mark, implicating him in Marlene's murder all those years ago.

In her bedroom, Dayna yanked her heavy suitcase from the closet onto the bed where she was raped. She packed it hastily, tossing in clothes without removing their hangers.

She emptied the bathroom trashcan to use as a vessel for gathering prescription bottles and toiletries before dumping them all into her suitcase. The zipper could barely close around all her belongings, but it did the job. There wasn't time to sort through everything now; that could be done later.

Thump by thump she made her way downstairs with the suitcase in tow and into the kitchen. From the house phone, she called Max, getting his voicemail.

"Hi, honey," she began, "I just called... I called to tell you that I love you more than anything in this world and the next. I wish things were different, but... I did what I needed to do, not what I wanted to. I'm so sorry." She hung up.

Tears welled in her eyes. She hadn't wanted to get her son's damn voicemail. She had wanted to talk to him, to hear his voice one more time. She wiped at her eyes. He would be okay... and hopefully one day he would understand.

Dayna reached for the receiver again and dialed 911. When the operator answered, she dropped the phone and left it off the hook. She slipped a large chef's knife from the drawer and stashed it in her purse for safekeeping. God forbid anyone stand in her way. She took a final look around the room, eyeing the stove to make sure it was off.

Old habits were hard to kill.

To think all this time, she had never thought to check the garage for Richard's car. It was there and now it was hers. The rev of the engine took her by surprise and she cheered as she reversed down the driveway in the car she was never allowed to drive.

Her cellphone vibrated in the middle console as she pulled onto the main road. She looked down—Sam. She longed to answer but knew that wasn't possible. She needed to keep her wits. She reached down and silenced the ringing.

She glanced at the dashboard clock. It had only been fifteen minutes since she'd left the house. Had the cruisers arrived yet? She pictured the red and blue lights bouncing off her white house, causing the neighbors to peer from their curtained windows. Maybe eventually they would gather outside on the sidewalk and speculate in hushed circles. Would the police knock on her front door or just decide to break it down? What would they make of the smashed mirrors? How long would it take for them to find Richard? What would they think? When would they tell Max? Her hands tightened on the steering wheel.

At the bank, Dayna smiled at the tellers and pretended everything was just fine and dandy as she withdrew $50,000 from her and Richard's joint savings account. Her smile never wavered as the teller counted it out before her. She ignored the stares from the other customers and a few of the tellers, proclaiming she was going to get herself a new car. It didn't matter what she said. She knew federal law required banks to report transactions over $10,000 in cash. The police would figure it out soon enough.

Back in the car, her cell vibrated again, flashing 'Sam' in the caller ID. He knew something was wrong. He was probably worried, given the state she had left in only a few hours ago. She appreciated his concern, but his calls could never be answered or returned. She chucked her phone out the window on Route 9. She didn't need it anymore.

Chapter 38

She pulled onto I-95 north in the opposite direction of the Green Garden Motel. An hour later she was flying past the 'Welcome to New Hampshire. Live Free or Die' sign. She chuckled to herself. Now she really was living free!

It wasn't easy to put her hometown and beautiful house behind her, but with each hour that passed and the distance from Richard's body grew, the better she felt. Her fingers relaxed around the wheel. She just might pull this off.

Max resurfaced in her mind. She shook her head and reached for the radio; distracting herself was the best option. She couldn't think about Max now. No sense risking something that might make her lose her nerve and head back to a ruined life and orange jump suit.

A loud bang shook the car. "Shit."

The car shuddered and went into a spin. A horn blared from behind her as she slid across the double line into the middle lane. A truck flashed on her right. Dayna jerked the wheel left, missing the vehicle by an inch, then back to the right where the car came to rest on the highway's shoulder.

She threw the car in park, activated her hazards, and exited. She circled to the passenger side of the car. The back tire was in shreds.

"Great," she said, wrinkling her nose against the smell of burnt rubber. "Just great." First one car, then the other.

It seemed Richard was already haunting her. He wouldn't even allow her to drive his precious Porsche from the grave. What was she going to do now? It's not like she could just pick up a phone and call Max—or even Sam.

Moves needed to be made fast if she had any hope of outrunning the police. She popped the trunk and removed Richard's emergency roadside kit. She searched through it but couldn't see anything in the dark. Out of frustration she dumped the contents of the bag onto the pavement. The items clattered out: some flares, jumper cables, a wrench, a tire jack and some other tools she couldn't identify.

She turned back to the trunk and struggled to remove the spare tire. After a brief fight, she freed it and propped it against the car. The tools were spread out before her, but who was she kidding? She didn't know the first thing about changing a tire. Maybe she could get the jack under there, but then what?

She began to pace. Someone had to come along eventually. All she had to do was position herself out front. After all, she was an attractive, middle-aged woman. A motorist would stop and ask if she needed help, wouldn't he? She'd prefer it be a woman, seeing she wasn't much into trusting men these days, but women were too wary to stop.

Anticipation grew as a car approached, the headlights momentarily illuminating her. It flashed by without slowing. The same thing happened with the next three passing cars. Finally, the fifth car, a black BMW, slowed and pulled off behind her. A man, as she predicted, opened the door of his BMW and walked towards her. He left his car running, the headlights blinding her.

"You need some help, ma'am? It's dangerous to be out here on the highway at night. I barely even saw you," the man said.

The guy, middle-aged with thinning hair, seemed harmless enough. He wore a nice suit that concealed a budding beer belly. A bright blue tie poked from beneath his suit coat. It looked a lot like the one she had given Richard on his last birthday. Her throat went dry. His hair was dark like her husband's, too. It had thinned more than Richard's, but the shade was exact. She swallowed. "My back tire's blown and my phone's... my phone's dead."

The man smiled at her. "Let me take a look," he said, a strain in his voice as he bent down and fished through the spilled items from the emergency kit. "Hmm. No flashlight: that's weird.

"Wait, hold on." Dayna opened the front passenger door and rummaged through the papers and pamphlets in the glove box. Then she remembered she had a small flashlight in her purse. She grabbed her bag and hurried back to the man. She set her purse on the trunk and dug for the flashlight, halting when her fingers brushed the smooth edge of the chef's knife. Jesus. Taking it by the butt end, she moved the knife aside, found the flashlight and handed it to the man.

"Thanks," he replied. "It'll only take me a few minutes to change the tire."

"I'd really appreciate," Dayna said, sighing in relief.

The man got to work setting the jack beneath the car frame. His blue tie glimmered in the headlights. "Cars really are such a pain these days. Porsche's are great cars, but even they aren't made like they used to be. Just the other day in fact, a friend of mine..."

Dayna stopped listening. She couldn't tear her gaze from the man's tie. It was just like Richard's. Hadn't he been wearing it that night he raped her? Dayna stumbled back. Her vision darkened and she reached for the trunk to steady herself.

"I told him he'd been ripped off good. Alternators go for maybe $600. Can you believe it? I should've had my mechanic buddy look at it, but..."

Dayna nodded, trying to respond to the man's rambling conversation. The tie caught her eye again, dangling in front of him as he worked. The world seemed to flip. She was no longer standing on the side of the freeway with a stranger, but in the bedroom watching Richard thrust into her from behind, his blue tie swinging above her as she cried out in pain.

The man stood and turned to her, his face a blur. Dayna took a step back and reached for her purse, ready to bolt.

"Whore," the man said. "You got what you deserved, you fucking whore."

"What?" Dayna asked. She blinked, and the world shifted

again.

"I said you're all set," he replied.

Dayna shook her head. She was gripping her purse in front of her chest like a lunatic.

"You okay?" the man asked and took a second step towards her.

Dayna stared at the tie again. She wanted to scream at him to stay the hell away from her, but her throat was too dry.

"I'm not sure what you want to do with your old tire. Let me lift it into your trunk for you." He took another step forward.

He was too close. Her heart pounded violently in her chest.

"I might need a hand, if you don't mind. The old back isn't what it used to be." He chuckled and took another step towards the trunk, right where she was standing.

Her hand plunged into her purse, searching for the knife.

He was inches away now. She pictured him slamming her against the trunk, acting out his wildest perversions.

"Please, stay away from me," she tried to choke out, but her words shook and jumbled together. Her fingers enclosed around the knife's end.

"It's no problem," he began. "Let me just—"

She plunged the chef's knife into his abdomen and jumped back.

The man fell to his knees and grasped the handle of the knife. He looked down at the weapon, then peered up at her in shock and surprise. "W... why?"

She frowned at him. As if he didn't know! He was just like her husband, nice now, but later...

He sank down to his knees. She was standing between him and the car, shifting from one foot to the other. His face in the full glare of the headlights became Richard's. He slumped and toppled onto his side, his cheek against the graveled shoulder.

She stepped to him and withdrew the knife, looked at it a moment, then wiped the blood onto his tie. Skirting his body, she tossed the knife through the open passenger door onto the floor mat. She caught sight of her reflection in the Porsche's side mirror. The dark woman looked back. A feeling of ecstasy and freedom washed over her. She had saved herself, acting in time to prevent a rape, if not hers, then certainly another innocent woman's. *This* was her calling. *This* was what she was supposed to do.

Dayna glanced at the Porsche, then back at the idling BMW. Now was the time to move, to leave Richard and his car behind. She scoured around for her purse, finding it near the Porsche's back bumper, then walked to the BMW.

She had to move the BMW's seat forward in order to reach the pedals. She pulled back onto the highway, casting a final look at Richard's white Porsche and his surrogate lying on the shoulder of the road beside it.

A hot feeling spread into her chest. How many other women would eventually come to the same conclusion she had? That Marilyn had? How many would learn that they were married to a monster, then have their lives shatter around them? She supposed it didn't matter. Just like it didn't matter anymore if the dark woman was the one responsible for the gruesome acts Dayna had committed. She didn't need answers or excuses anymore. As Sam said, ghosts couldn't make you do anything you didn't *really* want to do—and that was good enough for her.

COSMIC
EGG
BOOKS

Cosmic Egg Books

FANTASY, SCI-FI, HORROR & PARANORMAL

If you prefer to spend your nights with Vampires and Werewolves rather than the mundane then we publish the books for you. If your preference is for Dragons and Faeries or Angels and Demons – we should be your first stop. Perhaps your perfect partner has artificial skin or comes from another planet – step right this way. If your passion is Fantasy (including magical realism and spiritual fantasy), Metaphysical Cosmology, Horror or Science Fiction (including Steampunk), Cosmic Egg books will feed your hunger. Our curiosity shop contains treasures you will enjoy unearthing. If you have enjoyed this book, why not tell other readers by posting a review on your preferred book site. Recent bestsellers from Cosmic Egg Books are:

The Gawain Legacy
Jon Mackley
If you try to control every secret, secrets may end up controlling you.
Paperback: 978-1-78279-485-1 ebook: 978-1-78279-484-4

Mirror Image
Beth Murray
When Detective Jack Daniels discovers the journal of female serial killer Sarah he is dragged into a supernatural world, where people's dark sides are not always hidden.
Paperback: 978-1-78279-482-0 ebook: 978-1-78279-481-3

Moon Song
Elen Sentier
Tristan died too soon, Isoldé must bring him back to finish his job… to write the Moon Song.
Paperback: 978-1-78279-807-1 ebook: 978-1-78279-806-4

Perception
Alaric Albertsson
The first ship was sighted over St. Louis...and then St. Louis was gone.
Paperback: 978-1-78279-261-1 ebook: 978-1-78279-262-8

Readers of ebooks can buy or view any of these bestsellers by clicking on the live link in the title. Most titles are published in paperback and as an ebook. Paperbacks are available in traditional bookshops. Both print and ebook formats are available online.

Find more titles and sign up to our readers' newsletter at
http://www.johnhuntpublishing.com/fiction
Follow us on Facebook at https://www.facebook.com/JHPfiction
and Twitter at https://twitter.com/JHPFiction

Printed and bound by PG in the USA